Dog Days

Short Stories
by

Beverly Delidow

Published by Black Dogs Paw Print Press
5 Rissa Ln
Huntington, WV 25704

Paperback first edition

ISBN 978-0-9979445-0-1

Printed in the United States

For
Jesse, Leah, Luke, Balto, Chiquita, Duchess, Beau, Spotty,
Brandy, Mischief, Lucky, and JJ

Truer hearts the world has never known.

A word of thanks:

I am grateful for the support of many wonderful people as I worked on these stories. A thousand thanks and a bark out to my writing group, the Black Dog Writers of Huntington, WV: Matt Wolfe, Brenda Evans, Jen Grover, Eileen Schley, Melissa Shepherd, Susan Maguire, Judy Freshwater Polak, and Llewellyn McKernan. Y'all are the best. A giant hug across the miles to my girls in groups: Janna, Annette, Jeannie, Christie and the Ta-Da BIC Brigade; and Robbin, Beth, and Amanda in our "explorers" club. My heart is always warm when I am with you. Hugs, wine, chocolate and a bushel of gold stars to Meggin and Erin – you have walked with me while I learned to be all of myself.

As ever, the love of family and friends sustains me. The animal companions who have shared my home gave me inspiration, love, happiness, and the ineffable beauty of wholehearted trust. My heart belongs to: Goblin, Tico, Coco, Callie, Elijah, JJ, Jesse, Leah, Balto, Luke, Chiquita, Harlow, Jessica, and GinnyBear.

Table of Contents

A Note to the Reader

This collection came into being in April 2015 during Camp NaNoWriMo. If you've never checked out the lovely people at NaNoWriMo and The Office of Letters and Light – do it. They're a blast. NaNoWriMo is National Novel Writing Month. It's actually international and participation increases every year. The regular NaNo slot is November and comes with a fixed target of 50,000 words in one work of fiction in 30 days. The April "camp" is less structured; you choose your target and your project. I have a saltatory brain – it loves to jump around – so I chose to write short stories. I decided to center the whole thing on the presence of dogs in our lives (and of us in theirs) because dogs have been on my mind.

I've shared my home with animals since childhood. Once I was out on my own, I adopted my first cat at 19 and never looked back. I didn't adopt a dog until I had a steady job and a house with a yard. And then came Jesse, a bright, funny, mischievous husky with bicolor eyes and a big grin. She was loving and loyal and the most wonderful friend. My tribute to her is the last piece in this collection. When Jesse was about five, Leah came along – a retriever mix puppy with long silky fur and soft brown eyes. My two girls teamed up with the neighbor's beagle, Duchess, and became the neighborhood trio. Everywhere I walked, I had three dogs with me. I'm still known as the dog-walking lady.

When we lost Jesse to illness at age ten, Leah and I shared our heartbreak. A month later, a friend found a big black goofy hound wandering his neighborhood. And thus, Luke came into our lives, all 90-some pounds of him. He took some time to adjust to an all-girl household and Leah schooled him about manners a few times, especially around meal etiquette.

Darling girl. She was gentle and reserved, always loving. She and sweet, silly Duchess spent their whole lives together; they even left us the same year.

For a year or so, Luke was an only dog, a free-range hound with a big grin and a bizarre habit of stealing raw English muffins. And then came Balto – a 75-pound husky shepherd mix with the same one blue eye that Jesse had. He was gorgeous – all black with a little white chest patch and white paws, long legs, and a magnificent sweep of tail. He could stand up, put his paws on my shoulders and look me (or lick me) straight in the face. We were all completely smitten. He would play with Luke so hard we called it ThunderDome and they would both fall dead asleep for hours afterwards.

He was deeply loyal, and once got himself through a cat door to get to me. He loved to run – we called it flying husky time. When he got away from me one September evening and didn't come back, it was devastating. I looked for him for weeks and weeks, went through every bit of road and woodland I could get to. There's never been a sign of him. More heartbreak.

And then came Chiquita. I've always had big dogs – Jesse was the "smallest" of them at 55 pounds. The winter after Balto left I was beginning to feel like I wanted another dog and I wanted a husky. I kept going to the shelter, looking for the right match. Well, the universe had another idea. A Jack Russell terrier mix puppy showed up in the woods along the road to the house. Hello, little miss.

She's no bigger than my cats, though her personality is much larger. She's the only one of the dogs that hasn't been mostly black. She is smart and funny and adorable. And she is definitely a DOG – this pint-sized, bat-eared ball of fire thinks she can run deer. She's broken four cable leads meant for dogs twice her size to try it. My boys, Luke and my younger cat, Elijah, thought she arrived just for them. The older cat has taken longer to warm up to this whippersnapper, but they both sleep with me. It's a happy household, if on the "fuzzy" side.

So that's a roundabout way of saying that my dogs ground me. They are the down-to-earth spirits that remind me what it is to love and live in the moment. In the evenings my two chase each other up and down the hall – a tiny white bullet and a big black galloping hound. She is barely bigger than his head and he is so gentle with her. It is sweet beyond words to see them both so happy. In these stories I want to celebrate the good that comes when we allow dogs into our lives, the moments they make us stop and notice, the ease with which they find and give joy, the complete way they give themselves to us and to the now. It is a gift to share your life with dogs.

1. The First Real Day of Spring

Six am, Toby's feet hit the porch, shuffling a little in his slippers as he fumbles half awake with the lead. Chester bounces at the other end overjoyed to be in the world of breezes and smells. The dog skitters in a circle around Toby's legs and then lunges for a squirrel shaking its tail across the street in the Grables' yard. Toby hasn't a chance. He hits the porch the way newspapers did when he was a boy. He can just remember the sound, a whump, and then a creak as his mother opened the door to pick it up. Now the "whump" is his hip and the creak is his knees and he groans as he slowly stands back up, holding off Chester who has left off conversing with the squirrel to poke his muzzle in Toby's face, snuffling and licking him.

Mary Grable comes out in her bathrobe with a watering can and waves. She calls out, "You OK, Toby? Did he get you again?"

Toby is too out of breath to shout back across the road. He heaves himself fully upright with his hands at his knees, sways a moment, nods and waves back. This is not Chester's first rodeo. Toby smiles at Mary, who smiles back, then turns to her planter boxes, leaving him to ease down the three porch steps and then meander in the yard after Chester, who has finally quit lunging and is now

1

sniffing everything within reach, as if he has not lived here for eighteen months and has not sniffed all of the same things every morning for all that time. Some days Toby gets impatient with this game and he just wants Chester to get on with it and do his business, so Toby can go back inside and sit down in his chair with a cup of coffee and berate the morning news guy on TV.

Today it's OK, though. The half dawn of an April day is rippling down the block. There's a scattering of open doors and muffled footsteps out to mailboxes for the paper. Delivery boys don't toss them anymore. It's likely a semi-retired fellow in an old green sedan making the rounds at four am, shoving the Trib into mostly the right mailboxes, not even rolling them the way Toby remembered. Toby used to get the paper, but when Angie got sick he just didn't have time and after that he just wasn't interested. It took him a long time to be interested in anything again. But then Chester showed up and there was no other choice but to get interested.

Toby follows the dog to the back corner of the yard where two maple trees stand at the lip of a small ditch where water sometimes runs. Chester runs his muzzle over a few sticks and then squats. When he finishes, he comes to sit at Toby's feet, looking up expectantly. Toby smiles at him and pats his silky head.

"OK, boy. Let's finish the chores and get breakfast." Toby uses a small plastic bag to pick up after the dog, tying it off and dropping it into a waste can at the corner of the garage. Having heard the word "breakfast", Chester is now the model of decorum, trotting at Toby's ankle as if he's showing at Westminster. Toby half smiles and shakes his head. Silly mutt.

They go back inside, with a final wave to Mary, who waves back. Toby washes his hands and scoops out a cup of kibble for the dog. He mixes in a little canned food and puts it down in front of Chester, who is watching him. The dog tucks into his food as if it's the first he's ever seen.

Toby is smiling as he slowly gets some toast and finds a jar of marmalade in the fridge. He wonders at Chester's exuberant innocence, greeting each new day as totally unexplored landscape. He wonders if a person could ever have that, too. To be so in one moment that the last one and the next one don't exist. He steps back and gives his head a quick little shake. Where the hell did that come from?

"Well, I just blew my one idea for the day, didn't I?" He laughs at himself while Chester concentrates on getting the last licks of food from his bowl.

Toby takes his two slices of rye toast with marmalade and a cup of coffee into the living room. He puts the coffee down on a side table and picks up the remote. The TV flickers on and fades from a diaper commercial to the morning news show, well-coifed people divulging the state of the world. Sometimes Toby wonders how they manage to know. Other times he thinks they really don't and they're just dancing as fast as they can.

He settles into his easy chair, Chester at his feet gnawing on a rope toy. The news people laugh and it sounds like barking. Chester looks up, then looks at Toby and cocks his head. Toby laughs and reaches down to run a hand over the dog's ears. Chester goes back to chewing.

Toby finishes his toast and sets the plate aside. He slips down in his chair with his coffee resting on his midsection, half watching the news, half watching the street as his neighbors set off for work and school. Seven-fifteen on the dot, the phone rings. He deliberately waits for the second ring.

Toby is grinning as he picks up the handset and answers, "Hello."

"Took you long enough, old man."

"And I'm worth waiting for, whippersnapper." They are both laughing. Grayson is Toby's daughter's oldest, sixteen, all elbows and eyeballs.

" 'morning, Pops. How's it going?"

"It's goin', Gray – I'm still on the right side of the dirt!" They both laugh. "How's that driver's ed going? You got your permit yet?"

"Yup. Drove Dad to the store yesterday. That was fun." Toby chuckles and they chat for a few minutes. Then Grayson hands the phone to Marguerite and heads off to school.

"Hey, Dad. How are you?"

"I'm fine, honey," Toby knows what's coming and he's not pleased with Mary Grable.

"Mary said you fell hard this morning. Are you OK?"

"Yes, really, I'm fine," he's trying hard to keep the exasperation out of his voice. "Chester wound his leash around my feet and then took off after a squirrel. I'm not some dithering old invalid! I can walk my dog without the neighbors nosing around in my business!" Toby's getting hot under the collar and he's trying to keep a lid on it. It's not Maggie's fault.

"Sure, Dad – of course you can. Just wanted to make sure you were OK. Last summer when Gumby knocked Dan over, he got a bruise the size of a baseball and needed stiches."

"Yeah, I remember that – looked like he'd been run over. But Chester only comes up to the ankles on that horse of yours." Toby is teasing her now. Gumby is a harlequin Great Dane with no sense of size or place. He towers over Chester.

"Oh, Dad," Maggie laughs, too, relieved.

They chat for a few more minutes and then say goodbye. Grayson will be over with a weed whip for some yard work after school. Toby plans on sweet-talking her into letting the boy drive him to the local Shake Down for a burger and fries. Just thinking of Gray growing up makes his eyes well up.

"Aw, crap, Ches – I'm turning into a sentimental old fool."

The dog looks up from his spot on Toby's feet. "She would be proud of him, is all. I wish she were here to see that boy take his first drive in the old truck."

Chester nuzzles his hand, then goes back to snoring with his chin on Toby's slipper. Toby ignores the news and stares out the window. He watches as a green and white lawn care van pulls into Mary's driveway. A tall, husky, uniformed man gets out and Mary greets him at the door and he goes inside. Toby blinks twice before he is willing to believe what he knows he is seeing. She has ditched the bathrobe and is wearing something dark and lacy and she puts her hand up to the man's cheek and the man's hands are at her waist. And then the door shuts and Toby is left with imagination.

"Lord. She better hope the rest of the neighborhood ain't as nosy as she is!" Toby shakes his head, thinking of Martin, Mary's accountant husband, five-foot five in boots, and a hundred-forty pounds dripping wet. "Poor guy. Wonder if he has a clue."

Toby shakes his head and shakes off any more wondering about what the heck his neighbor is up to. He reaches for a pair of drug store reading glasses, sitting on the occasional table next to his chair. He puts them on, then reaches again for a medium-sized soft paper book of crossword puzzles and an erasable blue pen. He always enjoys this quiet time – brain stretches, Angie called it.

As he's about to start the flutter of a curtain catches his eye, blown out a little by a puff of air from a heating duct. He looks at it, peering over the glasses low on his nose. Slowly, his head turns taking in the rest of the room. It suddenly occurs to him that he's living in a house decorated by a woman. This is not really news. Angie had free rein of all sartorial decisions in the house, including dressing the house. Toby has never had an eye for anything related to style or color – when asked to choose paint he would invariably gravitate to white or various shades of beige. Once he shocked Angie into startled laughter when he pointed to a sweet pale shade of barely robin's egg blue. It was still on the walls of the bedroom they had shared for 36 years. It reminds him of her love, girding the walls and filtering into every corner of his life. Chester is the first addition to the house more significant than a light bulb since she's passed.

Toby sits with the puzzle book in his lap contemplating that thought. "Don't dwell, abide." One of her little sayings. It pops into his head now; he can hear it in her voice. She always teased him about being the ruminative one in their marriage. If it had been up to him, they might not have lived in this very house – he'd wanted to "look at a few more", wary of making the wrong decision. Angie had laughed at him and shook her head and pointed to the tulips blooming along the front walk. "This one, Tobias. I want this one – I want these very tulips and I want our kids to play on this lawn." He melted. He did every time. They bought the house. They raised their two daughters. Sent them off to start their own lives and their own families.

Toby sets the puzzle book and pen back on the table. He stands, folding the glasses into his shirt pocket, and steps to the front window. He looks at the walkway. The tulips are long gone – the bulbs dug up by an industrious squirrel some years ago. It's April – not time to put in bulbs, but Toby knows what is needed. He turns and chirps to the dog.

"Come on, Ches. Let's go get some flowers for mama." Chester stands, stretches and wags his tail, looking expectantly at the hook by the door with his leash. Toby smiles at him, and goes to the bedroom to get socks and shoes. The local nursery has been advertising hyacinths in pale Easter basket colors. She always loved them. He imagines them waving their silly heads in the curving bed along the walkway, sending up that perfume that always reminds him of chocolate eggs and sugar cookies. He picks up his keys and Chester follows him out to the truck.

Toby gets in, checks his mirrors and adjusts the rear view – the fittings have been loose for years. He starts the truck, glances side to side, and then looks up at the mirror as he pulls the gearshift into reverse. Foot on the brake, he reaches up and pulls the belt across his body, then buckles up and lets go.

🐐🐐🐐🐐🐐

2. Music

Blazer woke from a dream, yawned and stretched, then lifted his head to look around. Dreama was standing at the counter in her going-away clothes, the everyday ones, not the long time gone ones. The jangle of her keys had stirred him out of sleep. He scrambled to his feet and trotted to her, hoping for one more treat, or maybe a quick strut around the yard before she left. It was boring when she wasn't there. And his ears had keyed in on the sound of a distant squeaky garage door. Maybe Cleo was out. Lovely Cleo, with her waving tail and royal bearing, queen of his desires. When he wasn't desirous of the huge knuckle bone Dreama had on the counter. He stopped dead in his tracks and stared.

"Got your attention, did I, big boy?" She smiled at him and ruffled his ears. "One more potty stop, and then you can have this, OK?" She always spoke this way, the rise in her voice making him tilt his head, as if trying to figure out what she meant. She let him out the backdoor into the fenced yard and he made the obligatory circuit of the fence before marking a few spots and returning to her. She let him in and he trotted directly to the counter and sat, staring at the bone as if willing it to leap into his waiting embrace. Dreama laughed.

"Go on, bub. House time!" Picking up the bone, she waved her other arm toward the living room and his day den. Blazer followed her, head swiveling, never letting the bone out of his sight.

"OK, buddy. In you go."

Blazer scooted into his kennel and turned immediately, adoring eyes still clamped on the bone. She smiled and gave it to him.

"Good boy."

He closed his jaws around it and turned to settle into his favorite corner of the kennel pad, setting the bone down gently between his paws, he began licking it. He barely heard Dreama as she closed the kennel door and left. Even the sound of Cleo barking at a marauding cat down the block didn't sway him now. He had one mission: to gnaw this bone until it gave up its secrets, render it to grist for his gleaming canines, to honor his ancestors with the crack that released the marrow, and then sleep the sleep of the victorious. He chewed down one lovely gristly knob, then slept as the sun from the window warmed his fur.

It was later in the afternoon, about one sleep from the time that Dreama would come back, when he heard a noise outside the door. He lifted his head, copper-colored ears swinging. The doorknob rattled and the air felt wrong. Blazer half stood, hackles up, and let go a low growl, and then a loud bark as the noise continued. Then the door noise stopped and he heard people voices, ones he didn't know. Blazer barked and barked again and the noise and the voices faded. He heard running feet and another dog's bark. That one sounded like Rory.

The running feet got faster and there was people barking and then Blazer heard a yip that wasn't a dog yip. Rory was a chaser and a catcher. Blazer figured he'd caught one of the humans. He wondered for a moment what humans tasted like, then stuck out his tongue. He liked licking Dreama's unfurriness because it was hers. He couldn't quite imagine actually tasting human flesh. He vaguely remembered nipping her when he was only a few seasons old – she had squealed high and loud and he had given her many kisses to say he was sorry. It had tasted of salt and iron and her surprise. Not really food to him. Probably not to Rory either. Rory was nowhere big enough to eat a human – he was only as big as one of their shoe-paws. He just thought he was bigger.

The noises outside faded for a moment and then there was a loud high whine that was irresistible, coming closer and closer. The noise howled and Blazer howled back. It sang and he sang. The music was delicious, it struck the chord of doggish being, giving it voice, calling him to answer from the very depth of his soul. He was almost sorry when it stopped, even though it got very loud. He gave one last moan to thank it. A light flashed from the road outside and he heard a car engine now that the singing had stopped. Rory was still barking, too.

Then Rory's barking faded, and Blazer could hear human voices, quiet ones and louder ones. He heard the car that always brought Dreama. The car pulled into the driveway, but the garage didn't open. He heard Dreama's voice outside, excited. He whined. When that didn't bring results, he started barking, yelping really. That almost always got her going. He heard her voice get near the front door, then get farther away again. He heard more talking, then car doors closing. The singing car drove off. He yelped again, louder, until he heard the garage open.

Dreama came running into the room and flung herself at the kennel door as Blazer puppy yipped – he just couldn't help himself. He knew this was going to embarrass him later. Dreama let him out and he wagged and wiggled and jumped up to put his paws on her shoulders. She hugged him and made soft little sounds, and then laughed as he sniffed at the remnants of tears and licked her face; she almost never let him do that.

"Oh, Blazie – I would have just died if they'd gotten in here and hurt you." Blazer half wondered if "they" had something to do with the noises and the music, but he was too busy enjoying a thorough petting. He rolled onto his back and let her rub his belly. Then he bounced up again, realizing it had been a long time since his last trip to the yard and he had been busy. He trotted to the back door and bounded out when she opened it. He managed to get just outside the "uh-unh zone" before lifting his leg.

He was just about done when he heard a noise from the back corner of the yard, a tiny squalling. Curious, he turned and then flat out ran when he saw the huge winged thing start to drop toward the noise. He barked and the winged thing left, swooping tight over his head. The small thing kept on squalling; he heard Dreama yelling, too. He nosed at the source of the noise – it was white and barely bigger than his paw and had tiny pin-pricky little claws. It looked like a miniature version of a cat, but Blazer had never seen a cat this small. He wondered if it was a new kind of squirrel.

The little white thing wobbled on its legs and Blazer sniffed it again. It smelled vaguely of milk and litter smells. He decided it needed a mama. His mama. He put his mouth gently over the tiny creature and lifted it. Head high, he trotted back to Dreama and dropped it into her waiting hands, then stepped back, and watched.

Dreama started making little "oh! oh!" noises when she saw it. She touched it all over and nuzzled it and then cradled it in her shirttail. She reached out to pet Blazer.

"You are a good boy! Such a good boy! Rescuing this poor little thing! What a day!"

She gave his muzzle another rub, then turned to go back in, carefully shielding the little pointy creature that was now making a sort of buzzing sound. Blazer got as close as he could to sniff at it.

"Careful there, bub. This little guy has had enough adventure for one day. And I have, too. Gee golly Crash Willikers! Or something like that." Dreama was muttering to herself now. She rarely used the bark-words other humans sometimes did.

Blazer followed her into the kitchen and sat to one side watching as she found a basket and a soft towel and made a nest for the little white thing. She set it in there and then warmed some milk for it and watched as it lapped the milk from a saucer. Blazer came over to see, snuffling. This made the little white thing squeak and puff all up. Oh cool! Blazer was fascinated – he sniffed again and got a tiny prickly paw tap on his nose. He hopped backwards and sneezed. It didn't exactly hurt, but it startled him. Dreama laughed and then reached over to pet him.

"Sorry, bub – it's been a long day and that was just funny." He nuzzled her hand for more petting.

Eventually the little white squirrel-cat went to sleep in the basket and Dreama carried it to the corner of the kitchen and gently set it down, saying, "uh-unh!" as he started to go sniff. Blazer backed up. She made her people food and gave Blazer his dinner nibbles with an extra biscuit. He munched it all down and lapped some water, then trotted into the front room to curl up on his soft bed.

What a glorious day! He got a bone, and something to bark at, and there was music, and chasing the flappy thing, and treats. And a pointy squirrel-cat. Maybe he could play with it again later. He fell asleep, just barely snoring.

Blazer woke a little while later, feeling something warm moving against his neck. There was that funny rumbly noise and tiny pin pricks and he could smell the squirrel-cat, but he couldn't see it. Then he heard Dreama cooing, "Awwww, that's too cute!" She knelt and petted them both, a gangling copper Irish setter with a tiny white kitten curled under his chin. Blazer felt the warmth from her hands and the little knot of the kitten curled up now licking a tiny paw... and his chin. He thought he might rumble too if he knew how.

🐈🐈🐈🐈🐈

3. Chase

The pack was in agreement – it was Ralphie's turn to forage. This didn't please Ralphie, but he knew turns were important. He also knew that Gibby would nip his hindquarters if he didn't go out and at least try to score something edible. And then it would be cold comfort around the den for a couple days. Gibby was as tall and skinny as he was short and squat, so she had the advantage when it came to being haughty. He set his head high off his shoulders and trotted off, undercut jaw grinning rakishly as he sniffed the air for any clues.

They had been sleeping in a den under a bridge for a few days. There weren't any humans there now, though there had been. One had left a tattered piece of cloth that was prized among the pack as a sleeping spot. So far only Dotty and Cap had gotten use of it; Dotty as official matriarch (though she hadn't whelped any of them) and Cap as her unofficial mate (unofficial because – well, he had lived with humans, and it happened, y'know…). Ralphie knew Gibby was angling for a shot at the blanket and that if he brought back good forage their chances were better. The pack needed to eat and China, Simpkin, and

Chewie were a bit young for stealth. They were also inseparable and mischievous, not good for scoring food.

Ralphie wasn't good at sneakery either – being a bulldog he looked like a fireplug, but couldn't hide behind one. He had to rely on looking like he belonged and he was on his way somewhere. With his short brindle-spotted coat he didn't look like a no-person dog, so if he trotted like he knew where he was going and ignored the inevitable chirps and whistles of people trying to get close to him, he was usually OK. He'd had to dodge a skinny guy with a bad face and a long pole once. The guy was driving a van and Ralphie could hear a panicked retriever in the back. That didn't sound good. Ralphie had scooted under a low fence into house yard and then turned and barked as loud as he could at the guy. Bad-face guy had looked up and down the road and then took off. Then Ralphie found a nice bowl of cat food on the back steps. He did leave a little for the cat.

Now he stomped his way along toward the park closest to their den. Sometimes groups of kids would have picnics and would toss food if he cocked his head. Sometimes he could score a whole package of food things if he was cautious and the people weren't. Ralphie entered the park woods following a deer trail and wound his way to the edge of the ribbon of trees that ran along one border, parallel to the creek at the other side. He sat still and scouted the possibilities. He saw several lady-people with the rolling boxes they put their young in. Sometimes the pup-humans were good to follow because they dropped stuff. These seemed to be asleep, so he kept scanning. A large herd of bigger pup-humans and a couple grown ones was seething and squealing by the metal toys. That group was too big for Ralphie. Too many grabbing fingers. He shook his head.

Moving just inside the wooded edge, Ralphie walked the length of the park checking out the prospects. One solo human sat on a bench with a bag of peanuts, cracking them and tossing them to the pigeons and squirrels. Ralphie like the taste of peanuts, but they were a big pain to get out of

15

the twiggy-tasting outsides. He used to chase the pigeons and squirrels when he was a pup.

He stopped, suddenly remembering that nugget from his pup-hood. He had been born in a people home and had lived with some nice humans for a while. Was it from chasing the squirrels that he lost his people? Ralphie shook his big head, ears flapping, and let the shake run right back to his tail. Didn't matter now, did it? He had a pack.

He kept moving, leaving the peanut person behind. A small hill rose between the woods and the creek, partially hiding the path and benches where people often hung out. Ralphie relied on his nose to tell him there was little of interest on the other side. He briefly gave chase to a squirrel that wandered into the woods. It scrabbled up a tree and he moved on. He was getting tired.

Ralphie sat down next to a big tree and rested for a minute. Sometimes on these forays he'd find a cozy place to nap for a while. After what happened to Ranger, they didn't sleep in the park. Ranger was asleep in a sunny corner, thinking he was safe, and a group of pup-humans scared him awake. They cornered him throwing rocks and sticks and he tried to run away. One of them grabbed him and he nipped at the arm that was hurting him. A big man-human with a stick came and caught Ranger and took him away.

Chewie had been on patrol with him and was hidden so he saw all of it. Ralphie shuddered. He knew that pack rules were that you backed up your mates, but self-preservation won out when it was many humans against one dog. Chewie was quiet for a couple days and stayed at the den. Then life moved on. China swore that she and Simpkin saw a dog that looked and smelled like Ranger way across town once. They couldn't get close enough to talk to it. That was past; finding food was now. Ralphie kept going.

And then – there it was. The most amazing food smell he had ever smelled. Big nosefuls of it; he figured the food must be hot or it wouldn't send up so much smell. But it was incredible – cheesy and hot-doggy and doughy. He had no idea what this was, but his mouth was watering. Ralphie edged around the tree and looked toward the smell. A man was sitting on a bench with a pup-human and its carrier. The pup-human was loose and tottering around. Next to the man on the bench was a large square. The man lifted the top of the square and the delicious smell wafted out; Ralphie realized the square held the food. The man started to reach for the food when the pup-human started running away from him toward the creek. It fell and made a loud wail. The man closed the square and ran to the pup-human. He scooped it up in his arms and brought it back to the bench. It made sad noises for a few minutes then went off playing again. Ralphie watched this with some interest.

The man opened the box and took out a wedge of food and began eating it. Ralphie knew he needed to work fast if he wanted to get some. He knew human young were chasers. They liked things they could run after. And toy things, especially. Ralphie didn't have any toy things. But the big group of bigger pup-humans had been playing with a ball. Ralphie was thinking that was too far away to go get when he looked around and could not believe his dog-luck. There, in the woods near him, in a pile of leaves and brush, was a ball. It looked a little dirty, but it was still round and Ralphie bet if he could get it rolling fast enough the pup-human would chase it.

He pawed the ball loose from the leaves and sticks around it and nosed at it. It rolled. He pushed it to the edge of the woods and looked around carefully. There was a lady-human pushing a pup-box. Ralphie waited until she was well past the man. He crept out, pushing the ball to the top of the small rise. He saw the man sitting on the bench and the pup-human playing on the grass nearby. He shoved the ball out toward them and it started rolling. It rolled right past the bench, getting faster, and the pup-human ran after it. The man was eating some of the food, so it took him a minute to notice, but then he got up and made a noise and started chasing after the pup-human again. Ralphie waited until the man was several human lengths from the bench before he launched himself toward it and the marvelous smell.

He barreled toward the bench, one eye on the pup-human chasing the ball and the man still chasing the pup. Ralphie ran around to the front of the bench, clamped his jaws over the square and took off back toward the woods, holding it up so it wouldn't drag. He heard the man shout at him when he was almost all the way into the woods, but he knew the man couldn't follow with the pup-human. As Ralphie wove his way into the woods, he heard a lot of people-barking, but he knew he was safe. So far. If he could get the food to the den, the pack would eat well tonight.

4. Audition

Calpurnia woke slowly in the same room, at the same time, every morning. Every day, no matter the weather, was gray and edgeless, bleeding into all the other grey, edgeless days. This day was no different. She opened her eyes, looked at the window, dawn blooming beyond the sheer curtain. A bird was chippering, most likely from the branches of the dogwood tree. She pressed her lips together and moved with deliberation. She threw the blanket back, one foot, then the other venturing out of the cocoon of sleep. She pulled a light pink bathrobe from a hook on the back of the bathroom door and put it on. She shoved her feet into a pair of worn slippers and willed herself down the hall to the kitchen.

A beam of sunlight broke free and poured in the kitchen window. Calpurnia filled the kettle with water and put it on the stove. As she did every morning, she put a spoonful of loose tea in a strainer and set it next to a teapot and a mug. A ritual inherited, along with her name, from an aunt back in England. Her father's oldest sister, a quiet woman of steely resolve, Calpurnia remembered her beautiful garden and determined singlehood. Aunt Cal was not one for dalliance.

Calpurnia wouldn't mind, but no one had made the offer in some time. Not since Myron? Marco? Marcus? Lord. She couldn't even properly remember his name. Though she didn't suppose it mattered. They'd gone out a few times over the course of a month one summer. She remembered going to community theatre production of "Anything Goes" in the high school auditorium. The performance had been creditable, the conversation stale and stilted. He called once after that, but she didn't return the call. Life drifted on.

That was several – more than several – years ago now, back when Cyrus was still a pup. Calpurnia glanced over at him asleep on his bed, legs flung long, just barely fitting on it, though the thing was practically as big as her couch. Well, not really – it just seemed like it. He did fill up a room. She told visitors that her living room was decorated in "Post-Modern Canine Candid". It contained the couch, one small side chair and a cabinet housing her television and a compact stereo. A couple folded tray tables leaned against the wall in one corner. The rest of the space was taken up with two large dog pillows, a kennel, and a scattering of half-chewed bones and toys. Cyrus put the fur in furniture, she joked. Even with a slipcover that she pulled off only at the last minute when guests came, the couch always seemed to be full of strawberry blond retriever hair. She didn't mind. She always came home to someone who was glad to see her.

As if on cue, Cyrus woke with a sneeze, a small explosive "wuff!", and then yawned and stretched. His looked up at Calpurnia and immediately trotted to her side, leaning against her hip and lifting his head for her to rub under his chin. He rumbled appreciatively. He'd always done that; it wasn't a purr, more like a prolonged grunt. It was sweet. Calpurnia ran both hands over his soft fur, then ruffled his ears. Cyrus stepped expectantly over to his bowl, and she filled it for him. Seeing that the water dish was almost empty, she rinsed and refilled that, too.

She guessed her own breakfast should come next. Calpurnia wrinkled her nose, opened and closed cabinets and then the refrigerator. Pickings were a tad slim. She had some rather geriatric cereal, but no milk or yogurt. There was one egg. Some frozen chicken parts. A bit of wilted lettuce. And for some reason an entire package of chocolate chips.

"Good lord," she muttered. And thought, not for the first time, that if the dog chow people would make people chow, she would be tempted by it. Just for simplicity's sake. No more decisions. No worries about leftovers. No dragging out to restaurants all the time. She sighed.

"Oh well. How 'bout it, Cy? Wanna come with me to the drive thru? We'll go to the park afterwards."

Cyrus looked up from lapping about a quarter of the water in his bowl and dripping another quarter all over the floor. At the word "park" he began barking and running back and forth between the basket that held his leash and the garage door.

Calpurnia half-smiled and shook her head. "Just askin'," she threw up her hands in a 'slow down' gesture. "Gotta give me time to get semi-presentable." He sat down by the garage door and waited expectantly, watching her. When she turned toward the bedroom, he grumbled and trotted back to the living room to chew on something. She hoped it was a toy.

Calpurnia went in the back to take a quick shower and put on weekend clothes. She was done in fifteen minutes, hair wet and slicked back, wearing a pair of jeans and a fleece pullover, good to go. She figured she had to come back to bring Cyrus home anyway, she could change into work clothes then. Or not. A tiny seedling of rebellion sprouted in a vacant lot somewhere in the back of her mind. She decided to ignore it for the moment and get on with the plan. She was suddenly very hungry and was not interested in anything other than getting to the Park-n-Perk and getting food. She picked up Cyrus' leash and whistled to him as she grabbed her wallet and keys and headed for the door. He was at her heels in seconds and bolted down the steps to stand prancing and whining at the car door.

"OK, OK," she shook her head as she opened the door for him and he lumbered up into the back seat. She patted his rump to get his tail in, then shut the door. She walked around the car and got in, hitting the remote for the garage door before putting the key in the ignition. Daddy's lessons were still intact after all the years. She backed out and started down the street. Then realized she didn't have her phone. She paused at a stop sign and looked back at Cyrus who was sniffing out the cracked rear window. She shook her head at her own internal debate.

"Screw it," she said under her breath. Cyrus stuck his head over the seat and sniffed her ear. She waved him off and turned on the radio. The public station she usually listened to came on, but talk radio wasn't going to do it today. Calpurnia was tired of talk. She tapped the buttons until she got to an oldies station, stuff she'd listened to as a girl. "Satisfaction" came on and it suddenly blistered her that Mick Jagger was on the oldies station. Good lord – when did *that* happen?!

The Park-n-Perk was an old burger joint that had decided to take advantage of the infatuation with fancy coffee and started serving earlier. Calpurnia wouldn't touch coffee with a ten-foot pole, but their breakfast biscuits were a guilty pleasure. She had intended to go through the drive-through, but it was lined up. What the heck, she thought. She pulled into a parking spot by a speaker and waited. A few moments later, blatting noises came out of the speaker. Calpurnia had no idea what it said, so she just proceeded as if it had asked to take her order.

"Good morning. I'd like a biscuit with fried apple and a large orange juice, please." She looked at Cyrus in the mirror. "And a sausage biscuit and a large water, too." Why not let him live a little large, too?

More noises came out of the speaker and Calpurnia just agreed. There wasn't any way to translate whatever the person was saying, so she was going to do whatever was necessary just to get food – pretty much any food – fast. Now that they were here and there were cooking smells, she was famished.

"Y'know what, Cy – I might just nick your biscuit and only give you the sausage. That's how hungry I am." Cyrus didn't seem worried. He panted and smelled all the smells at the window.

Blessedly, a server arrived within minutes, bearing a tray with three biscuits, orange juice, water, and apparently two coffees. Calpurnia rolled down her window for the girl to hook the tray on, paid and let the server scoot back into the building before she looked the unexpected bounty before her. She was bewildered at first, then it hit her as ridiculously funny. She was giggling as she sorted through the biscuits and found one with apple, one with sausage, and one with both apple and sausage. She laughed out loud, "Guess you don't have to share your bikky, love." Cyrus barked in agreement and she turned around to ruffle his ears and to unfold the paper wrapper and lay the sausage biscuit on it for him. His eyes got saucer-sized and he downed it in seconds, then spent the rest of his time lovingly licking the paper.

Calpurnia decided to live dangerously and try a sip of the coffee. The miserable brew her mother had made at home had turned her off all varieties years ago. But this stuff actually wasn't bad. It was hot, not burnt, and the bitter edge kind of tasted good, especially after she added the two little plastic cups of cream to it. She folded back the wrapper of her apple biscuit and took a bite. Flaky, salty biscuit and sweet, cinnamon-y apple melded in her mouth and she closed her eyes and sighed in contentment.

"Oh God, that's good." Color crept into her cheeks and into the world. She thought maybe this was the first thing she had tasted – really tasted – in a very long time. And there was no real reason why. She looked at the clock on her dashboard, 8:10. She wasn't due at work until 9:30; another clerk was opening today. The old line from "Mary Poppins" about people in cages popped into her head and she realized that she had no intention of going there today. Maybe not ever again.

This thought hit her straight between the eyes. Calpurnia stared, unseeing, out the front window with the biscuit in her hand and her mouth open, frozen mid-thought and mid-motion. She laid the hand with the biscuit in her lap and sat very still for a moment. The words came out of her mouth, "I don't like doing this and I don't have to."

"Sorry?" Calpurnia jumped. She hadn't seen the server come back to the window.

She waved off the girl's concern at having startled her. "It's OK – I was practicing my lines."

"Are you in a play?"

"No, more of an audition, really. Not a public thing." Calpurnia marveled at her own improvisation. More, that it was true.

"Well, good luck! Are you through? Would you like a carrier for these?" The girl pointed to the extra coffee and the water.

"Sure, thank you." Calpurnia waited for the cardboard carrier, then dropped a couple singles on the tray before the server whisked it off. She poured the water into a small bowl she kept in the car for Cyrus and gave it to him. Then tucked the coffee into a carrier slot and laid the unopened sausage and apple biscuit next to it. That seriously had the look of a picnic lunch. But maybe not for a while. She had finished the first coffee and she felt a little buzzy.

She finished the last few bites of apple biscuit and looked back at Cyrus, who was standing in the back seat.

He was watching a group of girls walk by with a Dalmatian puppy. He wagged his tail and whined.

"OK, doggo – let's go to the park." He gave a yip and she started the car.

5. Minding the P's and Q's

Sean and Didi sat in the tree house and watched as Saturday morning got rolling around the neighborhood. Lundys were doing yard work. Mr. Venkata was pruning roses, shadowed by Princess, a little white Chihuahua. Petersons were washing their car, suds flying everywhere because Mrs. Peterson seemed kind of mad and Mr. Peterson was still teasing her. Sean and Didi giggled when she turned the hose on him "accidentally", and then tried to stifle their laughter while laughing harder when the adults turned to look around for the source of the noise. They both held their breath, Didi whacking Sean when he tried to break her concentration by making faces at her. The Petersons went back to rinse and revenge, flinging water at each other when they thought no one would see.

"Gawd," Didi whispered. "They're as bad as the twins." The twins were Sean and Didi's six-year-old sisters. They were a combined force to be reckoned with, but they didn't combine forces often because they were always bickering over silly stuff. At 9 and 10, Sean and Didi were beyond such things. Mostly. They watched for a while, munching on some grapes and cereal squares Didi had thought to bring up. Once the Petersons were done washing the car and had gone in, they nodded to each other and started down the ladder. The Petersons were right next-door and, while Mr. P. was pretty cool, Sean and Didi knew Mrs. P. was fussy. Especially when she was already mad. No sense poking that beehive.

"Quarton children! What were you two doing up there?" Mrs. Peterson's voice was loud and mad. They didn't realize she had come out to roll up the hose. Didi was pretty sure it wasn't any of Mrs. Peterson's business what they were doing in their own tree house, so she stood her ground. Sean looked at his shoes. Didi smiled at Mrs. Peterson and said "Hi, Mrs. P. We were hanging out. C'mon, Sean. Mom wanted us to watch the girls, 'member? 'Bye, Mrs. P." Didi waved and Sean followed her into the house. When they were safely inside Didi turned and whispered, "Nasty old bat," in his ear and he cracked up.

Mom came out of the kitchen with Jeremy on her hip. His face was covered with smeared jelly and he was babbling. She shook her head at the two giggling in the front hall, "You two!" she laughed. "Have you been up to no good?" She poked Sean in the ribs on the way by as she went to answer the phone.

"Hello…. Oh hi, MaryJean. How are you?"

Sean and Didi looked at each other wide-eyed. That was Mrs. Peterson.

"Uh-hunh…Yes. They're big kids. They're allowed out there whenever they like. … Why, no. I have no idea what they talk about up there. Why would I?... Uh-hunh… Uh-hunh… Did they shout anything? … Did they throw anything? … Were they making faces or something? … Hanging out – well that sounds about right. So what's wrong? … Look, MaryJean. It sounds like you've had a hard morning. I'm sorry you're having a rough time. But two kids laughing in their own tree house is just that – kids laughing. I don't know if they were laughing at you or me or the Reverend Sun Young-Moon. And what's more, I'm not going to ask! ... If they never showed their faces and didn't actually do something inappropriate, then they didn't cross any lines.... Well, I'm sorry you feel that way, but no, I will not tell them they can't go up there and we are certainly not taking it down. Tom spent four months building it and the kids love it. ... MaryJean, we don't have an association and we checked with the city. There are no zoning rules for tree houses... Look, MaryJean – I have to go. I have a jelly-covered nine-month-old who needs changing."

On cue, Jeremy started babbling loudly "Bah-Bah-Bah!" and put one sticky hand on Mom's face.

Mom gestured to Didi, who came and took the baby from her. Mom mouthed "thanks" and "it's OK".

Mom continued to say "No" and "Uh-hunh" at regular intervals. Didi figured she'd hedge her bets. She wrapped both arms around Jeremy and carried him into the kitchen. He was too big and too squirmy for her to hold on her hip, so she set him on the floor and got a wet paper towel. She dabbed and swiped at the jelly as well as she could while trying to make a game of it so he wouldn't fuss. She got a little of it off.

Mom came in with Sean trailing her; she said a final goodbye and clicked the phone off. She set it on the counter, and moved toward the cupboards, one hand on her hip, she rubbed her face with the other and muttered "Nasty old bat". Didi clapped a hand over her own mouth and ducked her head, but Sean snickered aloud.

Mom half smiled and waved a finger at them "You two!" She opened the top cupboard and got down a pitcher. "Sean, would you get the big box of tea from the pantry? The red one not the green one, please."

He tromped over and came back with it. Mom opened the box, took out four teabags and handed it back to him with a smile, "Away, please." He tromped back. Mom put a kettle on the stove to boil the water and scooped some sugar into the bottom of the pitcher. Then she made sure

Jeremy was occupied with a teething biscuit and turned to the two of them.

"Ok, dynamic duo, let's hear it – were you actually doing anything nefarious in the tree house this morning?"

Sean started to protest, but Didi shot him a look and spoke for both of them, "Nuh-unh. We were just eating grapes and watching stuff."

"What stuff?"

"Mr. V was cutting rose bushes with Princess. Lundys raked up a whole bunch of leaves. Mr. and Mrs. P. were washing their car and there was a lot of splashing."

Sean snickered and felt Mom's eyes turn to him.

"Well, she sprayed him! It was hilarious!"

Mom cocked her head and gave them a knowing look. "So that's why she was all steamed up. She was embarrassed. Still not your fault. They were in their own driveway – anyone could have seen them."

She looked at both of them and put a hand on one hip, "Were you polite when she spoke to you?"

"Yes, Mom – really!" Didi made a cross-my-heart motion across her middle. "And we didn't go on their lawn!" Sometimes Mrs. P. got mad about that, too.

"OK. Good. Remember that some people like to be asked before you go across their yard." They both nodded. Mom smiled and said, "Now who's ready for some sweet tea and a tuna sandwich?"

Didi's face lit up, "Can we have pickles, too?"

"Yes," Mom was laughing now. "You two are the darndest pickle eaters I ever met! Sean, here are some plates for the table. Didi, please find your sisters wherever they are and get them to wash their hands."

They scrambled to their assigned chores and lunch around the big wood table was happily peaceful. Daddy came home halfway through, all sweaty from playing basketball. He pretended to smear them all with stinky sweat and Mom made him go take a shower.

In the afternoon, Didi and Sean were back in the tree house. The sun came in one window and Sean was lying in the warmth of it, half asleep. Didi had her notebook open on the small table and was sketching a picture of a gingko leaf she'd found, though she was close to dozing, too. They both looked up when they heard Penny barking and growling like a crazy dog. Penny was the Peterson's poodle. They hadn't seen her much recently. Didi peeked out the window and saw Penny jumping at Mr. Peterson as if she was mad at him. In his hands he held what looked like two tiny furry hotdogs. He ignored Penny snarling at him and set them down in a little circular pen on the lawn. Penny jumped in and started sniffing at them as they started to crawl around. Didi almost bounced out the window.

"Sean! Sean!" she hissed. "Come look! Penny's had puppies!!" She was whispering but she was so excited it almost came out as a squeak.

He opened one eye and both eyebrows sailed upward, "Hunh?!"

"Come look!" she gestured at him, pointing madly, but with short gestures so that her hand didn't go beyond the sill.

Sean sat up slowly and yawned as he ambled over. He looked out. The pups were so small they were barely visible in the grass.

"They look like worms," he laughed and made a face at Didi. She made a face back. She liked almost any live thing that walked or flew or crawled, but she thought worms were gross and disgusting.

"Gross out," she stuck her tongue out at him. "They do not – they look like tiny baby puppies and they are so cute!"

"If you like woooorrrmsss," he teased, almost in her ear.

She made the "ICK!" face again and almost bumped him away from the window with her hip, but decided not to. She ignored him instead.

Mr. Peterson looked up and saw them looking out and waved, "Hi, kids! Wanna see the puppies?"

"Can we?!" Didi's squeal was loud and almost out of the range of human hearing. Sean stepped back, and pretended his ears were ringing.

Mr. Peterson nodded and gestured, "Come on over. Just be careful of the flowers."

Didi nodded and they both scooted down the ladder. They stopped at the edge of lawn just to make sure, but Mr. Peterson wave them on, so they tiptoed around a bed of blue and pink flowers and then threw themselves into the grass next to the pen.

"Oh my gosh! They're so cute," Didi was enthralled. "How old are they?"

"Three weeks. This is the first time they've been outside," Mr. Peterson gently lifted one blond wriggling puppy and handed him to Didi. "This one's name is Pongo." She nearly swooned.

"Oooh," she cooed. "He's so soft." She laid her cheek on the puppy's silky fur as Penny sniffed at her and decided she was OK. Didi set Pongo carefully in her lap and stroked him as he tottered around.

"The darker puppy is Perdita," Mr. Peterson pointed to the second puppy trying to climb Sean's leg while he grinned. "MaryJean wanted to name them after that movie, you know the one?"

Didi nodded. She knew that the movie Pongo and Perdita were Dalmatians, but she didn't care. These puppies were so precious!

"They're wonderful!" she said, letting Pongo inch his way into the grass, making tiny puppy noises. Penny came over and nuzzled him and he nuzzled back. Didi thought she would melt.

A shadow fell across all of them from behind Mr. P.

"What are you doing?" Mrs. P. looked mad still.

"I brought the puppies out and asked the kids over, MJ. You know the vet said they needed to get out and start exploring."

"Well, that's just lovely. Don't forget we have things to do."

"Sure. We won't be long," Mr. P. tried to smile up at her but she stomped off. Didi watched her retreating back in surprise. She wondered if Mrs. P. was feeling bad – when Didi felt bad she was always really grumpy.

Mr. P. tapped Didi's shoe. "It's OK," he said. "She's upset because we've already decided that this is Penny's last litter. And once the puppies start going outside, then they're growing up. And when they're growing up, then it isn't long before they're big enough to go to their new homes. She always misses them when they go to their new people."

Didi nodded. "I would, too."

Mr. P. smiled at her, "I miss them, too. But Penny's had three litters and the vet thinks that she might not stay healthy if she had more. Besides – if we'd kept them all we'd have nine dogs! Enough for our own poodle sled dog team!"

Didi and Sean laughed. "Pretty small sled!" Sean joked. Mr. P. smiled and nodded.

They watched the puppies for a few more minutes, then Mr. P. said it was time for them to go inside with Penny, who was now trotting in worried circles around them. He let Didi carry Pongo up to the door for him and he disappeared inside with the pups, Penny at his heels.

"Bye! Thank you!!" Didi called after him. Sean just waved.

They scooted back over to their own yard, skirting the flowerbeds. The look on Didi's face made Sean wonder what she had cooking in her brain. She could get pretty creative. And goofy, as far as he was concerned. Some of her schemes had so many "and then if's" it was like a million to one odds. But there was that one.

32

She was wandering around the yard occasionally reaching out to cup her hand around one of the trees and then swing around it. One eye and one corner of her mouth were tucked up in concentration. Uh oh.

"OK. Spill it, Deeds," he poked her in the arm to get her attention.

"Ow!" She gave him a ticked-off sister look. "Spill what?" she pouted, rubbing her arm. He made a face; he hadn't poked her hard, she was just surprised.

"Whatever grand plan you're hatching. You got that look."

"Oh," she gave him the serious look now. "But you can't tell Mom and Daddy. At least not yet."

"Nothing illegal, immoral, irreparable?" Sean rattled off their mother's rules for what they were allowed to keep to themselves. He was the older sibling, after all.

Didi shook her head.

"OK," he said. "Spill."

"What if we adopted one of the puppies and the Petersons kept one? Then Mrs. P. wouldn't be as lonely for them and she could see them both almost every day. That'd be, cool, hunh? And we'd have a puppy!"

Didi's eyes nearly rolled back in her head at the thought. Sean knew that look. Infatuation and determination were Didi's special gifts. The family was in for a long campaign until they either had a poodle or the universe exploded, whichever came first. Sean wasn't betting on the universe. He remembered the campaign to go see dolphins. It involved a car trip, two hotel rooms, what felt like a forty mile slog over sand dunes, and a run-in with a huge guy who made the mistake of tossing a can on the beach in front of Didi. And she had only been 8 then.

"Uh-hunh," was all he said, nodding. "But, Deeds, you have to get Mom and Dad *and* Mr. and Mrs. P to agree about that. D'you think that's gonna happen?"

"I think I have a secret weapon," she grinned. And wouldn't tell him what it was, even though he grabbed her and tickled her hard.

"It better be good, that's all I'm saying." Sean knew enough to admit defeat and move on. She'd give him the rest eventually. And she'd probably be bossing him around. He rolled his eyes and started poking at a loose pinecone with a stick.

"It's good." Didi left him to his poking and wandered back toward the tree house. She had no clue what her secret weapon was, but she'd find one. It might even be Mr. P. She thought about the way he nestled Perdita in his arms to carry her back in. He liked the puppies, too.

If this worked out, Pongo would be sleeping in her room by the end of the summer. Didi smiled and climbed up to the tree house. She had work to do.

🐕 🐕 🐕 🐕 🐕

6. Moving On

Tracy looked around the living room and fought the urge to just scream. She was so tired and so frustrated and so mad, she wanted to kick a hole in every box and then throw them in the yard – all four hundred or however many of them there were. Every muscle in her body ached, her very eyelashes were tired, and the now-ex-boyfriend she had moved here to be with had just left yet another message about how he couldn't find his picture and did she maybe have it because he really wanted it back could she call him please. She didn't even know what the hell picture he was talking about. She had one poster from her college days and two small desktop frames with pictures of her parents and her nieces. There was no picture with him in it – not any more.

In love or in thrall, she had left her safe, known life and moved here with him, knowing no one and having no job. And he liked that. When she started to move out from their tiny circle of two he became angry. She did what she could until she could do it no more. She got a part-time job, earned enough for first and last, rented this little house and got out. By the end she didn't know who he was any more. She was pretty sure he'd never known her.

So here she was – unknown and misplaced; sitting in a pile of boxes, mostly books and a few pots and pans. With no idea what she would do next.

Tracy wanted her life back. She wanted the friends she'd left back in Heatherton, the job at the local paper, the little café where she always saw someone she knew. She wanted life to be a known quantity again. She sat down on a large box and let a few big, exhausted, weepy tears roll down her face. Sometimes being a grown up was too freaking hard.

The doorbell rang, startling her, while the corner of the box she'd been sitting on caved in, dumping her onto the floor. She squawked and then scrambled to her feet, thinking maybe it was the cable guy.

She scrubbed at her face with one hand and opened the door. It was not the cable guy. It was a guy. And a girl. And a dog.

"Hello…?" She looked at them puzzled.

The girl waved cheerfully, "Hi! I'm Wren."

"And I'm Penn," the guy smiled through a bushy beard. He didn't wave because he was carrying a box.

"And this is Pinochle," he indicated the dog who had eyes only for the box. Pinochle appeared to be a cross between a Shetland pony and a mop. But frizzier.

"We're your new neighbors, from the blue house over there," Wren waved a hand back and to the left. It was well past dark, so Tracy had no idea which one that was. She was a bit befuddled, since she had no place for guests to sit, but she figured she would be as hospitable as she could.

"Um, hi. I'm Tracy – uh, come on in. The moving van only left an hour ago. I haven't found anything but a few light bulbs."

"No worries," said Penn amiably. They all wandered into the living room and Tracy's assemblage of boxes. Wren quickly took stock, pulled one box over as a table and found a couple crates to use as seats. Then she trotted into the kitchen and came back with Tracy's mop bucket, which she turned over and claimed for herself. She pulled paper plates and napkins out of the bag slung over her shoulder and Penn set his box down and opened it, revealing a glorious hand-made white pizza.

"Voila!" he said with a grin as Wren reached back into the bag and pulled out a bottle of wine and some cups.

Tracy felt a little surreal, as if cameras were going to sprout out of nowhere and the host of some bizarre house moving show was going to wave a microphone at her and "get her impressions". But she pushed that feeling down, making an effort to be at least polite.

"This is amazing – thank you," she stammered.

Wren grinned at her, "You're welcome! Dig in! We love it when new people move in. New faces, new places." She and Penn touched cups and grinned at each other. They held their cups to Tracy so she bumped hers, too, and then they all dug in. Tracy realized she was ravenous.

"If this pizza is what happens when people move in, then I'm all for it." Tracy took a second bite and almost purred. "God, that's good! Do you make these?!" She looked from one to the other.

"Penn does. I do graphic design. What is it you do?"

Tracy rolled her eyes upwards, cocking her head and gesturing with the pizza slice. "Cub reporter slash ex-girlfriend slash aspiring writer slash barely employed." That was life in a nutshell. Emphasis on the nut.

"Just moved for the second time in six months, so I guess you could say I'm a professional boxer, too." Tracy gestured to the mayhem around them and they all laughed, Wren above the others, bubbling and chortling.

Pinochle sat a short distance away, watching them. When Tracy got up to find some paper towels to use as extra napkins, he loped after her into the kitchen.

"Hullo, dog," she said, looking down at him. He sat and solemnly extended a paw to her.

She shook it, "Pleased to make your acquaintance. I wish I had a treat for you. Been a long time since I had any doggy treats in the house." She let go of the paw and patted his head; his slightly mournful eyes shifted back and forth under a fringe of wiry hair, watching her. He was quite odd looking, but sweet. He sniffed at her hand, focusing on a smudge of olive oil from the pizza. She patted him again.

"Don't think so, bud." She got the roll of paper towel and went back to the living room, Pinochle trailing her.

She handed out paper towels and sat down again.

"You got yourself a friend," Penn nodded toward Pinochle, now sitting at Tracy's left elbow.

"He is rather sweet," she looked back at him and he licked her face.

"Ooph!" Tracy cracked up "He's a better kisser than the ex, too."

Penn said "Ouch!" and Wren burst into infectious laughter again. Tracy started giggling and almost couldn't stop. It was all so silly and so unexpected. Then again – if the universe hands you silly on a plate, you just can't say no. She realized that she was truly enjoying herself for the first time in ... she had no idea how long.

"Wow," she said that out loud.

"What?" Both heads swiveled to her.

"Really, thank you for doing this. I was just realizing that this is probably the most fun I've had in ages. Since well before I moved here with Michael. Poop head." She said the last part only half under her breath, out of habit, because she'd been calling him that nonstop for the last miserable week of rushing to find a place and packing and moving.

Penn was looking at her shyly. He was much quieter than Wren. He had endless brown eyes that suddenly got even darker and serious.

"Because of him? Did he do that?" Penn pointed toward the base of her neck. Oh crap, Tracy thought. Her t-shirt had stretched a little through all the moving and the last of a thumb-shaped bruise was showing. She took a breath and nodded.

"First and only time. I wasn't waiting for a second."

"Good girl," Wren got up and came over to wrap her arms protectively around Tracy. "My God, that must've been awful."

"Yeah," Tracy sighed. "Sucked."

Not to be left out, Pinochle scootched closer and put his head on her knee.

"Awww!" Wren exclaimed. "He never does that – He must really like you!"

Tracy smiled and patted the dog. "He is a sweet natured old thing. How old is he?"

"We don't know," Wren shrugged. "He's a foster dog. We have a couple Corgi's who are dog-friendly and I work from home, so it just kind of happened that we started taking in fosters from the shelter who needed socialization. Pinochle has been with us... how long is it, Penn?"

"About four months," he was nodding. "Pretty long time for a foster. They usually get adopted out, but he's big and funny looking and quiet, people overlook him."

"Aw," Tracy ruffled the dog's ears. "He's a good boy, he deserves a good home." Wren and Penn exchanged a look. The germ of a thought crawled into the back of Tracy's brain and wouldn't leave. It was telling her maybe Pinochle shouldn't leave either. She tried to duck around that inkling by returning to the conversation. But, of course, she had to ask about him.

"He's really sweet. How did he end up at the shelter?"

Wren patted her mouth with a napkin and started to speak at the same time as Penn. He gave her a furry smile and said "You first."

Wren nodded. "So – near as we can tell – his mother was a full-blooded Irish wolfhound and Poppa was not quite." She made a face. "So the owners had three pups they couldn't scam into shows and couldn't feed. They managed to find homes for the two smaller ones, girls, I

39

think. They stumbled along with this one for a while. The guy had a gambling problem – would bet almost anything in a card game. He was playing cards one night and the only thing he had left to bet was the remaining pup. Lost him to a fellow who dropped him right at the shelter on the way home. He said no way his wife would let him keep the dog and it was ugly and it had puked in his car, to boot."

She leaned toward Tracy, "Between me and you and the wall, I'd've puked in that car, too. The women at the shelter told us it stank of cigars and crummy leftover food in take-out bags stuffed under the seats. Ew!"

"So they were playing pinochle? Is that how he got his name?" Tracy asked, confused.

"No," Penn spoke up, with a lazy grin. "They were playing poker, but you can't name a dog 'Poker' – so we called him Pinochle. It just seemed to fit."

Tracy cracked up and Wren and Penn laughed with her. Pinochle put his head on her knee and stared up at her from under those ridiculous eyebrows. *Oh hell*, she thought. *I'm done for now.*

They finished eating and started to stack cups and plates together. Wren tucked two remaining slices of pizza into a piece of foil and gave them to Tracy for later.

"Thank you – this is wonderful." Tracy looked at the assembled used plates "I think I can find a trash bag, hang on a minute." She went into the kitchen, put her pizza in the refrigerator, and came back with a couple plastic bags for the trash.

She found Wren alone, gathering up the cups. She looked around, slightly forlorn. "Where are Penn and Pinochle?"

Wren waved toward door, "Out for a walk. Pinochle needed a potty break. They'll be back in a minute."

She smiled at Tracy and leaned in toward her as they worked together to bag the used plates. "He likes you."

Tracy smiled, "He's a sweet dog."

"Oh, of course Pinochle likes you, dear. I knew that right away." Wren patted her arm, "I meant Penn."

Tracy jumped as if she'd sat on a live wire. "Uh... ah ... umm," she stared at Wren, who was watching her with a half smile, head cocked. Tracy swallowed and managed to ask, "Isn't he your husband?"

Wren's laughter pealed out high and genuine.

"Oh gracious, no!" She actually had to sit down she was laughing so hard. Finally she managed to gasp out, "That's not legal in this state or any other. He's my brother. And Pinochle is not the only picky one in the family."

Tracy blushed and they both laughed. Penn and Pinochle came back in and they all sat chatting for a little while. For the first time in a long time, Tracy felt at home and at peace, even in the middle of the rubble of her former life with two near strangers and a very large dog who was licking her face again.

Eventually Wren stood and yawned, "C'mon, little brother. I have four projects I have to beat on tomorrow and Tracy must be done in."

He nodded amiably, bestowed another bearded smile on Tracy and chirped to Pinochle to put his leash back on.

Tracy walked them to the door. "Thanks very much – I can't remember when I've had a more wonderful welcome to a new neighborhood."

"You are very welcome," Wren said. "Here's our number. Call us in a few days when you get settled in." She handed Tracy a napkin with a phone number on it. Tracy nodded, Penn waved and then they were gone. She was suddenly exhausted and stumbled into the bedroom. She managed to get her shoes off before collapsing on the inflatable mattress and falling dead asleep.

She woke some hours later. Midnight sounds ticking around her. She wandered back out and stood in the middle of her disheveled living room and blinked, remembering the odd events of the evening. She didn't remember the last time she'd felt so at ease, even in the midst of chaos. She was suddenly ravenous. Straggling into the kitchen, she opened the fridge and saw the foil wrapper. She opened it.

Tracy picked up a piece of Penn's delicious pizza, saluted, and said, "To a new and wonderful life." And took a big bite.

7. Run

Carrie stood at the wall and stretched her legs. The small out-building at the Palm Street entrance to the park was where she always started her run. She looked around while hooking one foot in her hand behind her and bending her knee to stretch her quad. All the usual morning faces were there – the guy bouncing a yellow ball to a toddler, the two older ladies walking two doddery Pomeranians, the couple drinking their lattés on a bench with a pile of newspapers, a bored teenager wearing headphones and rolling his eyes while his parents power-walked and bickered. His eyes swept over Carrie and then came back and left again. He slumped on a bench, shrugged and disappeared into his music.

Carrie smiled to herself. The fact that a teenage boy even looked twice was amusing. She was probably twice his age and not much younger than his parents. She finished stretching, shook out her limbs, and started jogging slowly along the path around the "lake". It was more of a large pond, really, but it was pretty, especially now, in early spring. There were flowering crab apple and pear trees just starting to bloom. Daffodils had naturalized in a few places;

dozens of them tossed their frilly heads in a light breeze. It was still cool enough for a light jacket; warm enough to feel good in the sun.

Carrie sighed contentedly and settled into her usual pace – about 10% faster than the slow jog, if truth be told. Speed had never been her thing, but she did like jogging. She liked being outside without having to explain to anyone what she was doing out there. She liked the way her legs felt after a long run, twitchy and powerful. She liked being alone with her thoughts and without interruption – no people, no devices … no dogs.

She looked up from where she was sprawled on the path. A black lab had come barreling out of the water with a wet tennis ball and knocked her flat. His owner came running over.

"Oh my God, I'm so sorry! Are you OK?" She was tall and had curly blond hair tied back into a short ponytail, loose strands were blowing across her face and the bluest eyes Carrie had ever seen. She extended a hand to Carrie to help her up. Carrie got part way up onto one knee, then gratefully took the offer. Their palms met and she thought she would drown in the warmth of two hands together. The jolt that went through her nearly knocked her down again.

Apparently, her companion felt the same way. They stood within inches of each other, staring, hands still clasped, while the wet dog circled, and finally broke the spell by shaking off water in all directions. They separated and tried to shield their faces.

"Jasper!" his owner squawked. "Sorry. He's only eighteen months old and still really puppyish." She paused, then looked Carrie straight in the eyes and held out her hand again. "I'm Dakota Winston, and this is obviously Jasper, the very bouncy dog."

Carrie grasped the warm palm once more and shook hands, "Carrie Mackelor. Really slow runner, really bad bouncer."

"I think you were going just fast enough." They both blushed, though Carrie wasn't exactly sure why. They shuffled their feet. Dakota looked at the ground, then up at Carrie, tilting her head a little.

"Can I offer you a cup of coffee? Make up for my dog nailing you?" She pointed across the lake at a little cart that was often there.

Carrie sensed genuine warmth under the hesitation in her voice. Something said to say yes. So, even though she "never did this", she did.

"That'd be cool, thought you don't really have to – it was completely an accident."

"I'd be happy to, though," Dakota's eyes were magnetic.

"Could I run a circuit and meet you over there?"

Dakota nodded and waved and Carrie set off, turning back once to wave back at woman and dog.

Carrie was so confused and stirred up she could not think straight. She knew what she was feeling. She hadn't ever felt it like this before. She'd always supposed she'd never met the right guy. It never occurred to her that, not only was she looking in the wrong places, she was looking at the wrong people. Holy crap. The intensity of what she'd felt was glorious, the instant connection almost hypnotic. She had no idea what to do about it. Maybe Dakota knew. And maybe someone could clue Carrie in on her own identity, because she was suddenly wondering who this person was, walking – or running – around in her own skin.

All Carrie knew was that she wanted to know more. So she ran. A little faster than usual. When she was nearing the end of the circuit she heard a shout and then panting. She laughed when Jasper appeared at her side from out of the water again and began running with her, tongue hanging from a big doggy smile. She jogged up to Dakota who was waiting with two coffees. Carrie accepted one gratefully.

"Awesome – thank you!"

"Thanks for not minding my horribly mannered mutt!" Dakota said the last part while drying Jasper's head with a beat up towel.

Carrie just grinned, "He's OK. Seeing him reminds me of good old Belfry from back home when I was growing up. He was our neighbors' dog – black lab-ish, I think he was a mix. Happy as a clam and dumb as a post. He would follow us kids all day long and we'd have to show him where his house was when it was time for dinner and they were calling him."

She laughed remembering. Dakota gave her a funny look. "They named him 'Belfry'?"

Carrie laughed harder. "Yeah. Goofy, I know. Maybe he was always daft."

Dakota chuckled and gestured toward an empty bench with the cup in her right hand. Carrie noticed she wore a thin braided leather bracelet. It made her hand both strong and vulnerable.

They sat on the bench and sipped their coffee. Both turned and started to speak at once, and they laughed.

"You first," Dakota gestured.

"No, you," Carrie responded in kind.

"Well, we can't both go, we already tried that..." Dakota was grinning at her. "So – come here often?"

Carrie smirked, "Eeeennnhhh!" she made a buzzer noise. "Bad pick up line. Lose a turn."

Dakota blushed, but persisted. "No, really – I bring the dog here all the time, and this is the first time I've seen you running. Most of the other regulars I see all the time."

"OK," Carrie relented. "But only because you got me coffee." Somewhere in the back of her mind she was thinking, *Are you FLIRTING?!* She hid her confusion by taking a sip. "Actually, yeah, I'm here a lot. But this is the first time I've run the lake path in a while. I usually head the other way."

Dakota looked at her, puzzled. "Why?"

"Fewer people, more hills."

"So basically you're saying you're a masochist..." Dakota grinned again. Carrie snorted.

"Most runners are." She rolled her eyes. "But, really, I run pretty slow, so I try to stay out of the way of the rabbit-types who often use the lake path."

"So, what made you switch it up?"

"Spring. The flowering trees. Daffodils – it's pretty."

Dakota looked out over the lake and nodded. Then she flashed a smile toward Carrie's side of the bench, "Glad you did."

Carrie blushed, but nodded and smiled back. She cleared her throat.

"So, when I'm not jogging into the path of oncoming canines, I teach part time at the U and take night classes."

"In what?"

"Law school. Always wanted to do it. Got a history degree, started at a big law school. Couldn't manage the financial burden. Had to get at it a different way. Working out OK. I'm more interested in small time stuff than clerking at the high court."

"Wow, that's pretty intense," Dakota hesitated. "I'm – uh – actually a carpenter." The way she said this, it seemed she expected things to go downhill after that, but that she was too honest to want to hide it.

Carrie's face lit up, "Oh, that's cool! What kinds of things do you make?"

"Mostly I restore wooden furniture that needs repairing. Try to match the missing pieces, or replace something that's cracked. I – uh – actually went to school in art history. Left before my senior year. I wanted to work on furniture, not talk about it."

Carrie nodded. "Don't blame you. Being able to create or restore something beautiful must be really nice."

"Yeah. It's cool. I've done a little work for museums here and there. Mostly I have private clients and a couple of antiques dealers I work with."

"So do you have a shop or a studio? Some place you work out of?"

"I have a full woodshop in the garage at my house." She flashed a smile again. "Picked the right parents. Dad was a serious hobbyist when I was growing up. Had every woodworking tool known to man. Or woman. I used to hang out with him when I was a kid. When he decided to retire and spend all his time traveling, I got the shop and the tools."

"That'd be really special – to use tools that were in your family." Carrie looked wistful.

"You don't have stuff from your folks?"

"I never knew them. They had me when they were very young, so they didn't have a life established yet. They were still in high school, were killed in a car wreck coming home from the senior prom. I was only a few months old. My mother's parents raised me. They were already older and had all they could do to keep each other going. They did the best they could. They both passed away when I was a teenager. I've been on my own since I was sixteen."

Dakota was staring, open-mouthed. "Oh my gosh, that's rough! You don't have any family?"

Carrie shook her head. "Not that I know. My parents were both only children. I think my father's mother may still be alive, but I've never met her. Seems Grandmother may have had a sister; I remember a few phone calls. It could be I have great aunts or cousins somewhere, I don't know. I've always been just my own little twig of a family tree."

"I can't imagine. I have an older brother and a younger sister and we all live within a few blocks of each other."

"Wow. I don't even know what that would be like. Must be wonderful!"

Dakota nodded and smiled, "It's pretty cool. Maybe you could meet them some time. They'd like you."

Carrie started to reply when her pocket started buzzing loudly. Startled, she pulled out her phone and looked at it.

48

"Oh shoot," she rolled her eyes. "I'm sorry - Excuse me a minute. This is someone from work." She knew what this was likely to be and she wasn't pleased.

'Hello... Hey, Jack.... Really? Oh, that's awful!... What? Are you kidding? This is the fourth time this semester! ... I know it's not your fault, but it's not mine either... Uh-hunh.... No. I can't.... No, Jack. I really can't. I have two appointments today that I can't cancel, so I'm sorry, but I can't teach your section for you. .. Yeah. ... No. I'm not going to be there today. This is my day off and I have appointments. You can always get one of the students to hand out a homework assignment. I did that for my class once. Uh-hunh... Yeah. Hope the little one feels better. Bye, Jack."

Carrie hung up, exasperated. Jack Brady was a full-time instructor in her department. He was also a full-time annoyance. He was always trying to pawn one of his sections of an intro course off on Carrie. She didn't mind in a true emergency, but this was the fourth time in six weeks and in the fall semester, she'd ended up having to take over one of his sections, and wasn't compensated for it. She wasn't doing that again. She sympathized if his kid was actually sick, but she was beginning to suspect he was just lazy. She put the phone on mute and put it back in her pocket. He'd been known to keep calling if the first time didn't work.

"Enough of that nonsense," she muttered.

"Problem at work?" Dakota asked.

"Yes, but it's not my problem, which is the problem," Carrie wrinkled her nose. "He's one of the full-time faculty, but he's always trying to pawn his intro classes onto the part-time instructors. Last semester I ended up having to take over one of his sections – ton of extra work and no additional money. I had to juggle my own classes to do it. The chair of the department knows about it, but he's too busy trying to help keep the College of Humanities together." She waved a hand. "University politics sucks –

what gets lost in the shuffle are the faculty who really care and the students. If that's the bargain they're offering, I'm shopping elsewhere."

"Really! That just rots!"

"Agreed. And – seriously – do they not realize how dumb it is to try screwing a future lawyer on the terms of an agreement? All they're doing is providing me with a sample case for my contracts class and grist for the day when I get mad enough to tell them to take their three classes for barely more than it costs me to park and file 'em!"

Dakota was grinning at her and Jasper started running in circles and barking. Carrie blushed and laughed at herself.

"Sorry – I do get a little wound up." She made a wry face, "They say academic politics are so vicious because the stakes are so small."

Dakota called Jasper to her and gave him a treat. "Can't blame you. Hard being on edge all the time. Do you have to go? You said you had appointments…"

Carrie's face grew warm again, "I was – um – exaggerating slightly. My two appointments," she used her fingers to make quotation marks, "are with my shower and my study partner. On my day off, I usually run a longer loop, get a shower, and then meet with Ramona over lunch to go over the latest from my law class." She shrugged. "I was not willing to give up my day, my study time, or a shower without a time limit to give Jack Brady an easy out. Again."

"Especially if all you get out of it is a bunch of extra work! That's ridiculous!"

"That's the fun of being in the ranks of the contingent," Carrie scuffed at a stick with her toe. "You get all the work and none of the perks of being on faculty. The one advantage is that they don't tend to put us on committees, so we are spared that circus." She gave the stick a final poke and it flipped upwards. Jasper leapt for it, almost landing in her lap. She pulled her coffee cup out of the way and laughed at him as he play-wrestled with the stick at her feet.

"He's so cute!"

"Yeah. Bit clumsy – but cute." Dakota hesitated a minute. "What time is it getting to be?"

Carrie fished the phone out of her pocket and tapped the button. Not only could she see the time. She could also see two missed phone calls. "It's 9:15. Need to get going?"

Dakota nodded, head down. She seemed to be thinking. "I've really enjoyed meeting you. I'm terrible at remembering numbers and I don't have my phone so I can't ask for yours. Could I give you my phone number?"

Carrie felt a warm little depth charge go off somewhere in the center of her chest and spread outward. She smiled and blushed and handed Dakota the phone. "I'd like that."

Dakota poked at the phone, one fingered, squinting. "We're having a cookout this weekend, me and the fam. Maybe you'd like to come? Casual – just some beers and burgers."

"That sounds awesome – I'd love that!"

"Great!"

They both stood there grinning like fiends as Dakota handed back the phone. Their fingers touched briefly and Carrie felt the warmth flare again. She was so charmed she wanted to swim in it. They stood there, smiling at each other, unable to move and unsure what to do next. Jasper settled that question by giving a yip and then barreling off toward a squirrel.

"Whoops! I better go get him!" Dakota started jogging off, turning sideways to call back to Carrie. "Call me tomorrow, OK? I'll give you the lowdown on directions and stuff."

"OK. I will – after my class, OK?"

Dakota gave a thumbs up and Carrie waved back. She watched Dakota catch up to Jasper and put him on a leash, then turn to wave at her once more. Carrie waved and then set off on a slow jog back toward her car. She had no idea where this was going, she just knew she was going to follow it as long as she could and enjoy every minute. If she was a different person than she thought she was when she got there – then that was probably who she was meant to be.

🐈 🐈 🐈 🐈 🐈

8. Royalty

Pippa paced the entry hall, furious. The staff had neglected their jobs again, so it was left to Pippa to wait for and announce the guests. Which she did. Loudly. Scrofulous bunch, if you asked her. Several of them had mud on their shoes. One even had – shudder to think it – cat hair (*CAT HAIR!*) on his trousers. Ridiculous.

After that indignity, Pippa turned her nose up and retired to her throne room. Enough of that nonsense. Let the nitwits below stairs figure them out without her. It wasn't just the guests they couldn't figure out, the lot of them were always calling things by their wrong names. Even Pippa. "Pippa" was just a nickname, but they couldn't remember the proper long ones so, it would have to do. Her mother had explained to her that one always allowed the staff to use the shorter names. It made them less anxious and error-prone. Pippa wasn't one to spare their "feelings", but she could not stand the squawking when they created havoc, so she put up with the whole embarrassment of the nickname.

Thus, Mademoiselle Princess Pippa-Sinestra Alegance was just "Pippa". Her mother, Queen Mother Pippi-Lunestra Alegrace, was "Pippi". The similarity made for some confusion among the less gifted of the help, but that was neither here nor there to Pippa. She only responded to the ones who spoke to her with the modicum of deference required. When she felt like it. The slovenly one who called her "Pipster" she simply ignored. That was quite beneath her, thank you very much, and she was not going to dignify such language with any sort of response. The slightly less scruffy one with the softer hands who prepared the bed very nicely was better. Pippa deigned to allow that one some latitude. She hadn't scolded that one for at least a day. The scullery maid on the other hand – by the Queen's Tail, that one was a trial to manage!

Pippa shook herself and rearranged her pillows to recline more comfortably. Even thinking about such a motley assemblage of dolts made her tired. She supposed they would have to do. Mummy was rather attached to them. The scullery one, especially. And even the other one who drove the carriage and did odd jobs about the house, though Pippa could not imagine why. Pippa had not yet forgiven that one for the disappearance of her brother, the young Prince Piper-Dextero Alagret. The driver dunce had taken Piper out for a drive one day, packed well with food and his little jacket, should it get cold, and even a comfortable cushion, should he need a rest. The carriage returned, but not Piper.

It was so long ago now, her memories of him were fading, but she remembered the sparkle in his eyes and in his smile, and his beautiful singing voice. Oh, that voice! Mummy said it was reminiscent of their father's. Pippa didn't know. As in all the royal houses now, once the queen gave birth and her blessing, her consort led his entourage to a second royal residence and took up there. She had never met His Majesty King Prosper-Solestro Alegent. Mummy said Pippa had her father's regal nose.

Pippa supposed she might meet Poppa someday; it was known to happen. She had overheard the daughters of one of the other royal houses chattering on Promenade Day.

They said they had been witness to a state visit, though they had no siblings to show for it. Their mother was so tiny it wasn't clear how she managed to produce offspring at all, so perhaps that wasn't surprising.

Pippa yawned. Whatever the other families were up to, she had some say about this one now and she realized she was hungry. She stretched and marched smartly to wake her legs up. She found the nearest staff member, the scullery one, and made her request politely, but firmly. Twice. Really, these dolts were too much. Thankfully, Mummy joined Pippa and helped to get a response from the poor dull thing. When, after an interminable wait, they were finally dining, Mummy admitted that the servants were slow, but she was so fond of them. She comforted Pippa of her impatience and assured her she would find the same tolerance some day. Pippa wasn't sure, but Mummy was a true Queen, so Pippa had hope.

After supper Pippa and Mummy strolled the gardens with two of the staff in attendance. Evening light played softly across the paths and hedgerows. Pippa stopped to bury her nose in an open blossom. Mummy kept slowly on, nodding to the staff and letting Pippa catch up on her own time. It was blessedly peaceful, the staff behaving for once. Together, queen and princess made a graceful circuit of their domain and returned to the parlor for a light snack before they retired for the evening, each with her attendant in tow.

Pippa sank into her pillows, saying a grateful-prayer as Mummy had taught her, for warm-ness and soft-ness and full-ness and fleet-ness. Drifting into happy dreams, she softly recited her full name, all eight glorious syllables, two for each leg, Pippa-Sinestra Alegance, Princess of the Royal House of Alegat, the highest of the Chihuahua royal courts. She slept and dreamed a royal dream.

9. Electricity

Lance woke up grumpy to the sound of running water. Before he was fully awake he launched himself toward the tiny bathroom to see what the hell was going on. Although, "see" was a relative term when he was half awake, didn't have his glasses, and tripped over the dog getting there. At least, from his position on the floor he could see that there was no water down there, so, for the moment – Lance was a realist, after all – he was safe; no leaks, no overflows, and it was just the commode handle that needed jiggling. He untangled himself from Murphy's laconic embrace (the dog was licking his arm) and bumped a few paces on his knees over to the bathroom door. He used the door handle and toilet seat to haul himself up.

Being that it was morning, and Lance had woken rather unceremoniously, he decided to take advantage of the facilities before trying to get the thing to stop wasting water. He lifted the seat, shooed the dog from his favorite water bowl, and took care of business. Relieved of several burdens, Lance flushed, washed his hands, and jiggled the handle in just the right pattern – four little shakes, then two – to get the thing to stop running again. He realized that his toilet had a combination, which made him laugh. Perhaps this day wasn't awful after all.

Milky light filtered through the kitchen window. It was raining again. Lance had lost track of how many days. He put on a kettle to boil and got the instant coffee out of the cupboard. He scrubbed his face with his hand and tromped to the pantry for Murphy's kibble while the dog sat politely next to his bowl and watched. Even sitting Murphy was formidable. He was a Harlequin Great Dane, with a hint of merle coloring in some of his spots. Seated, his head still came up to Lance's waist. He was fantastically even tempered, something Lanced admired and was at times deeply jealous of. He gave Murphy his kibble and got a box of rye crackers for his own breakfast. Grabbing the kettle before it started whistling, he spooned coffee grains in to a cup with some sugar and powdered creamer and stirred the hot water into the whole mess.

He gathered everything at the bar-counter and sat down. He peeled back the top of a can of sardines and pulled them onto a plate with a fork. Lance couldn't remember when or why he started eating sardines for breakfast, but he liked them, so he kept doing it. Sardines on rye crackers or toast had been his morning meal for years. Sometimes, he'd sprinkle a little vinegar on them, or soft boil an egg. His favorite was to have them on dark rye bread with a healthy smear of butter and a slice of onion. Today he was content with a bit of oil from the can and a shake of black pepper. He took a couple bites nodding, sipped his coffee, and sighed.

Lance looked out the window, which faced the side of the house, toward the front. The rain had tapered off and the cloud covered thinned. He could see Marjorie Pell getting her newspaper in a bathrobe and huge curlers. Did women still wear curlers these days? Hunh. Who knew? Lance didn't. He hadn't regularly shared quarters with a woman since he'd moved out of his mother's house some thirty years before.

"Then again, how could the ladies resist this, eh, Murph?" He patted his belly and looked at his plate and snorted. There probably weren't too many women willing to put up with fish for breakfast every morning. He shrugged and lumbered to the front door to get his own paper, Murphy at his heels.

Lance opened the front door with the intent of getting the paper off the stoop. Instead, he said "Waah!" and took a step back, bumping into Murphy. There was someone standing there. And she was a she. Lance stared. He couldn't remember the last time a woman appeared unbidden on his doorstep. If ever. He blinked. She was still there. Smiling. At him. In his bare feet and striped pajama pants and stretched out t-shirt and morning stubble. And she was quite a woman. As tall as he was, broad-shouldered and sturdy of carriage, square features below smooth blond hair pulled into a ponytail. She reminded him of his dad's old pictures of pin-up girls. Except that she was wearing an olive green uniform of some kind and it managed to be sexier than all those bathing suits and dresses. Geez. What the heck was he thinking? Meanwhile he was gaping at her and she was waiting patiently for him to notice her extended hand. In a daze he finally lifted his hand as if he had no control of it. She grasped it firmly.

"Good morning, sir! I'm Bernadette Hamilton with Lakeside Power. I'm the new meter technician in this sector."

"OK," Lance was baffled as to what a meter technician was, let alone why one wanted to speak with him. In his pajamas. "Um, nice to meet you," he manage to get out. "What can I do for you?"

"Oh, no, sir. We don't need you to do anything. I just have a couple questions. The company noticed increased use in this part of the grid. That sometimes means there's something on a line in the area. Have you noticed a difference in your electric bill lately?"

Lance thought a minute, scratching his head. "Well, no. Not particularly."

"Have any older appliances that seem to run a lot?"

"Noo… the 'fridge is pretty old but it doesn't run more or less than it always has. The water heater was new last year, and the heat is one of those heat pump things. It's less than ten years old."

She nodded as he spoke. "They're probably fine then. Any indoor plants?"

He gave her a funny look, "You mean like potted flowers?"

"Or anything. Sometimes people start their garden seedlings on a rack with grow lights. That can cause a jump in power needs."

"Oh. Nah – I just have a few bushes out back here, been there forever. Don't have time to fuss with things in pots."

She nodded again. Lance had a funny feeling it wasn't tomatoes Miss Hamilton was interested in. Years ago Lance might have had an interest in that, too. But life was pretty placid these days. The occasional beer was enough.

She seemed to run out of things to question him about, but still stood watching him. He scratched the back of his head again.

"You could check with the folks in the house with the red shutters," he pointed. "They had squirrels in their attic last summer. Maybe som'a them got into the wiring."

She thought about this for a moment. "That's possible. No problems like that for you?"

Lance shook his head and pointed to Murphy, "They don't like the company around here."

She gave a tight smile. "Right. Can see how they might feel that way. Looks like a fine dog, though."

"He's a good fella." Lance laid a hand on Murphy's back and Murphy leaned into him.

Lance thought she was fine to look at, but this game was getting old. He had no idea what she really wanted, but it was unlikely to be charming banter about squirrels and dogs.

"Do you need to check the meter or the wiring or something?"

"Meters were read on the third. But… If you don't mind, I'd like to get another reading to see if the use off this meter is at a normal rate."

"Sure. It's around the back between two big hydrangeas."

He started to ask if she'd like to come through the house, but she turned, and strode smartly toward the right hand corner of the house. Then came back and went the other way. The gate was on the other side. Lance went back in, got his coffee, and went straight back to the sliding doors in his kitchen, Murphy padding behind him. He opened the door and let the dog out before sticking his head out to look for her. He didn't see her, but saw the hydrangea moving. He stepped onto the cement patio strip, looked, and was treated to the sight of shapely olive-clad rump swaying gently as the top half of her worked her way through the two hydrangeas.

Lance was about to ask if he could help her by clearing some of that away when Murphy came right up, cocked his head back and forth at the rustling bush, and then poked at her with his nose. She yelled and backed out of the bush in a hurry. She came up, ponytail swinging, almost in a fighting stance. Murphy backed up and sat down, staring at her. She swept her eyes right and left and then settled on the dog. She shook her head and smiled.

"You're a sneaky one for such a big dog."

"Sorry about that," Lance said.

She jumped and blushed, "Oh! I didn't know you were there!"

"Sorry," he said again. "I went through the house." Lance pointed toward the bushes. "I didn't realize they were so overgrown – I can get the clippers and trim that back."

She nodded. "We'd appreciate it, sir."

"Sure. Gimme a minute." Lance returned to the house and pulled on a pair of jeans and a flannel shirt. He rummaged in the garage for his hedge clippers and went around back. The hydrangeas had gotten huge.

"Wow – had no idea these things had gotten so big." He'd been laid up for a while last fall; by the time he felt like doing anything, they'd already had snow, so he didn't think about doing yard work.

He clipped at a few branches at the front of one bush, then clipped deeper and teased the trimmed branch out. He repeated the process on the other bush. Dog and woman stood behind him watching. He continued working and, slowly, a path between the bushes emerged. As he clipped, the memory of summers with his grandfather surfaced: the hot days, lemonade and shade trees, and the beds of rose bushes, all waiting for his grandfather to shape them. Granddad had shown him how to judge what a bush would need, to trim the right spots and leave the right spots. Lance worked now almost by instinct, having absorbed his grandfather's lessons right to the bones and muscles of his hands.

He ran a thumb over the cut end of a branch, and reached, out of habit, into his shirt pocket for a glue stick. Not there. He stepped back and started to go around to the garage for it when he realized Bernadette was still there; his face colored.

"Oh, sorry. Kinda got into it and forgot you needed to get in there." He shuffled his feet, and looked down. Without thinking he had shoved his feet into his beat-up slippers, one of which had a hole in the toe. *Lord*, he thought. *You do know how to charm the ladies.*

He turned back to the hydrangeas and made another few cuts to clear the sightline to the meter. Then backed out and gestured to her. She nodded and brushed past him, taking a rectangular device of some sort from a clip on her belt.

He stood to one side and looked out at the yard to keep from eyeing her backside again. Looking at the lawn and the shrubs for the first time this spring, he could see that he had several weekends' work waiting for him. Maybe this was a good day to start. He was mentally calculating how much mulch he needed when she cleared her throat.

"Hunh? Oh sorry, got thinking," he smiled a little and pointed to the device in her hand. "That tell you what the problem was?"

"Gotta watch it – That thinking can be dangerous," she smiled back. Then shook her head, "No, sir. Seems there's no excess use at your meter. I'll have to keep looking."

It occurred to Lance that he'd like to keep looking at her; he rubbed at his face to keep from blushing scarlet.

She held out her hand again and he shook it. "Thank you, sir. You've been very helpful. The office will be in touch if anything else comes up, but I doubt it."

"You're welcome. Hope they figure it out."

She nodded and marched smartly around the house. In the wrong direction again. She was blushing as Lance watched her turn around.

"Um. You're welcome to come through the house," he waved at the door. "I always do that."

She hesitated for the first time in their brief acquaintance. "We're not supposed to impose, sir."

"Can't be an imposition if I invited you. It's no trouble at all," Lance stepped to the sliding door and opened it. Murphy went barreling through. Lance heard the skitter of big paws across linoleum and then heard him lapping water.

She hesitated, but then thanked him and he stepped to the edge of the door and waved her through. He turned, slid it shut and turned back, heat rose to his face again when he saw her looking at his half finished plate with a smile.

"Brings back memories," she nodded toward the sardines. "My Swedish grandmother loves pickled fish. Eats it at every meal and is going strong at 104. My grandfather fished for a living, so everyone in the family respected the fish." She said the last with a Scandinavian accent, smiling more to herself than at Lance. Then she blushed a gorgeous pink and said "Oh goodness, I apologize. We're not supposed to bring up our personal lives on the job."

"Nah, that was nice. I won't tell if you won't," Lance smiled at her. She smiled back and paused just a few seconds before she started toward the door.

"I won't take up any more of your time, sir." She handed him a small piece of cardboard was she walked, "This is my card. If you have any questions, feel free to call."

"Thanks," he took the card and opened the door for her. She turned on the stoop and shook his hand again and strode toward a grey van he hadn't noticed before. Lance watched her open the door, easily step into the high vehicle, and thump the door shut before she drove away. He looked at the card in his hand. He wondered what she would say if he called. And what she would do if he invited her to the fish fry at St. Leonard's next weekend. He blushed again, then turned to go in to finish his breakfast. Murphy was sitting just inside the door, head cocked, staring in the direction the van had gone. He looked up at Lance and gave a low whine.

Lance patted his head, "I know what you mean, Murph. We'll have to see what we can do about that." He wandered back to the kitchen and his breakfast. The last of the sardines tasted better somehow.

10. Team Spirit

'Drea stood on her front steps staring at the open door and the hole in the screen, trying not to swear, even under her breath, so that the toddler in the stroller would not pick up that language. Michael was so adamant that Keisha was not going to have a potty mouth. In the meantime, he was likely responsible for forgetting to close the door so that Bullet, so-named for obvious reasons, would not do what he had done before. And now had likely done again. She took a breath, said, "Yes, baby" when Keisha pointed a chubby finger at the door and said "Mama, wook!", and steeled herself to ask first and not assume there was blame to distribute. She wondered how long it would take to find Bullet this time. She lifted the stroller to the landing, picked up her daughter and went in, dreading the next few minutes.

'Drea stepped into the house and headed toward the unfamiliar sounds in the family room What she actually found was Michael happily wrestling on the floor with their dog. And a second fireplug of a pit bull. 'Drea stared open mouthed. Michael was laughing so hard he couldn't speak, so he just kept playing with the dogs.

Bullet looked like he had won the lottery. He was grinning, tongue lolling, head butting Michael and the other dog. Bullet was white with large black splotches. The other dog was brindle and white with a white patch over one eye and dark over the other. 'Drea already knew his name was Pirate. It just would be. He was rolling on the floor, wriggling in canine delight, panting and batting at both Michael and Bullet with whatever paw happened to be closest.

The dogs wound down and began just snuffling and lolling on the floor. Michael finally caught his breath and sat up. He smiled at her and shrugged, "Hey, Dray – this time one broke IN instead of Bullet breaking out!" And then he started laughing again.

She gave him a small smile and shook her head, shifting Keisha on her hip. The baby was leaning forward smiling at her daddy, but 'Drea was not going to put her down next to a strange dog.

"Broke in? Good lord! How did that happen?"

"I was working in the office and had opened the door for a little fresh air." He held up a hand when she gave him a look and started to say something. "I had him on a lead - he was fine. He would walk out to the door occasionally and sniff, but he wasn't trying to get out. He fell asleep in the hall. All of a sudden I hear barking and he bounced to his feet and he was nowhere near the door when this one came up, stared in through the screen, and let loose the loudest, most pitiful whine. I've ever heard. Then he disappeared for two seconds before he came running straight at the door and went right through it. He ran right up to Bullet and they touched noses and that's when Bubba-fest got going. I took the lead off so they wouldn't get tangled and they've been going to town ever since."

Michael pointed to the dogs now snoring, sprawled next to each other on the floor, smiling even in their sleep. "That's the happiest pair of dogs on the planet right now."

'Drea saw where this was going, and even though she already knew this dog's name and where he would be sleeping at night, she still had to put up a small defense.

"Oh no, Michael Manfield, we are not just taking some random dog off the street with the bad habit of running through doors. We already have a dog that runs through doors, do you think we need another one?"

Michael listened while getting himself off the floor and back into his chair. When she stopped, he smiled at her and said, "He may not be a stray. He doesn't have a collar or tags and he wasn't dragging a leash, but we know firsthand what a pit bull on a mission can do. The shelter is closed now, but we can take him over there in the morning and see if he has a microchip. I'll take a few pictures and put them online tonight, see if someone is missing him. His coloring is different enough someone should recognize him."

"Mmm hmm," 'Drea was somewhat mollified, but didn't want to cave to quickly. "Maybe so. This little girl needs a bath and some dinner." She nodded at Keisha starting to fuss in her arms. The little girl reached for her daddy so he came over to give her a kiss, "Hello, baby doll! Did you have a good play time?" Keisha nodded and pointed to the dogs "Who puppy, daddy?"

"We don't know, sweetie. He's lost, so Bullet played with him so he wouldn't be lonely while we find his people."

Keisha nodded, wide-eyed. 'Drea's arms were getting tired, so she hoisted Keisha again, "Ok, child, we gotta go."

Michael kissed the top of Keisha's head and then leaned toward 'Drea; she turned her head away, so he kissed her lightly on the cheek, then stepped aside. She felt a tiny flare of anger rise and then let it go out, like a match that didn't quite catch. She didn't want to feel like this either, but the habit was hard to break. As she turned she saw the two dogs, flopped on the floor in complete trust. She almost burst into tears. Instead she took a breath and took Keisha upstairs.

Michael called after her, "I picked up some chicken after the game – want me to put it on the grill in a bit?" Michael coached baseball; sometimes 'Drea even brought Keisha to the games, but it had been a while.

Watching her step on the stairs, she didn't look back, but said, "Do we still have some salad left?"

"I bought more. And some sweet corn, so we could grill that, too." From the top of the stairs she looked down at his eager face. He was trying. So hard. It was almost harder to forgive him that. *Give the man a little credit, 'Dray!* She gave him a tiny smile and a nod. "Sure, that would be nice."

He gave her a full-on grin and trotted off to start dinner. She heard both dogs skitter after him. She knew Pirate was home for good. Same way she had known Michael was staying in her life. When Bullet fell asleep in Michael's lap on their second date that pretty much sealed the deal. When it came to things like that, Bullet never steered her wrong.

'Drea was every bit the girly-girl growing up, and she still wore the hell out of a dress, with heels and makeup, flashing a killer manicure. It was part of her uniform as a contract attorney. So it always surprised people to learn that Bullet was her dog, not Michael's. Her law firm had sponsored an adoption event for the local shelter and she loved dogs, but had never had one, so she volunteered. One of the shelter staffers was taking her through the rooms full of dogs and they stopped in front of a cage with this half-grown pit bull with a big grin. The minute she saw him, she knew she was a goner. He was six months old then, with a silly sense of humor and a sweet nature and a face she could not resist. He ran to the bars separating them, snuffled at her hands, and then heaved himself onto his back so she could rub his belly. She made them put a big tag on his kennel before the event even opened –

"ADOPTED". That dog was not going home with anyone but her.

She didn't meet Michael until the following summer. He was coaching a peewee league baseball team. Shay, one of her friends, had a son on the team and invited her to a Saturday afternoon game. They chatted in the stands just behind the team's dugout while the kids scrambled around. At one point a player on the opposing team flung a ball toward third base, trying for a double play. The ball hit the runner, hard, in the back of the leg and he fell, sobbing in pain and surprise.

The umpire called a halt to play. Michael knelt by the injured boy and made sure he was OK, then spoke quietly to him for a minute, calming him. The boy's mother came running out of the stands in a panic. Some of the bigger boys watching started taunting. Michael looked up and locked eyes with the other coach, who looked away.

From where they were sitting, 'Drea heard everything that happened next. Michael helped the boy into the dugout and gave him an icepack for the bruise. He then called his team together.

"Guys, this is a game. Sometimes stuff like this happens. It's hard on Tony because he got hurt and it's hard on the team because he's our first baseman. Stuff happens. It's nobody's fault, and that means we don't try to get even and we act like it's over and done and we go on no matter what stuff happens. Because this is our game and we play like men. Right?"

The boys shuffled their feet and one red-headed boy started to say, "But, Coach, ..." Michael shook his head, "Nope. You know the rules, Chuck. We don't play for revenge. We play because we play – we play clean, we play fun, and we don't count up points. In the end they don't matter."

The boy pointed to the other dugout, "It matters to them."

"I know," said Michael. "That's why they keep losing, even when they win. We know better. I want you guys to play like that. OK?" They nodded. "Good. Now, your folks are here – do 'em proud!" He put a hand in the center of the circle of boys and they all put a hand in on top of his. They all yelled "Team, Go!" and flung their hands upward and the game went on.

Michael's team won handily and the opposing coach wouldn't shake his hand, even as two rows of eight-year olds managed that little bit of civility. Michael was laughing about it with the umpire when Shay and 'Drea walked by. Michael broke off talking, looked her straight in the eye and smiled. That was it.

They dated for six months; she introduced him to Bullet and her family, in that order. They moved in together and married a year after that. That was two years ago. 'Drea got pregnant before she was quite ready to think about a family, though Michael was elated. Her ferocious independence was challenged at every turn by parenthood. She didn't like it. But she would chew iron and spit nails if anyone tried to get near her child. Keisha was going to grow up healthy, strong, and unharmed, or someone would bear the scars of it. Michael called her Mama Griz, and marveled at her fire. She didn't find that amusing either. 'Drea's sense of humor seemed to have evaporated in the delivery room.

Maybe it was because 'Drea had been a latchkey kid, practically born independent. Not that she had a choice. Her parents both worked two jobs to get ends somewhere in proximity, if not actually to meet. The bare necessities were usually there, but exhaustion won out over affection in the house. 'Drea could remember her mother coming off of two eight-hour shifts, grey-faced over a cup of coffee in their tiny kitchen, falling asleep because she sat down to braid 'Drea's hair. Only Pop had been able to attend 'Drea's high school graduation, sitting on the aisle with tears leaking from his eyes. She knew he and Mama loved her, and were proud. She also knew it would be up to her from then on. 'Drea scrapped and scraped to get through college and then won a scholarship to law school. It gave her the first sense of ease she'd ever known, though it got dented pretty quick.

Mama's family had bad-luck genes, and she had smoked for years, doing whatever she had to to stay awake and keep working; she had a terrible stroke during 'Drea's first year of law school. 'Drea did what she could, got some rehab services, and helped her father cope. But then in the winter Mama got pneumonia and that took what was left of her. She died after a hard month.

'Drea's father lived on alone in their tiny flat, rattling around in forced retirement. Both jobs had let him go when he kept having to take time off to care for his wife. His sisters took meals over and 'Drea called every Sunday. As often as she could, she'd make the drive over there, feeling strange in her old haunts in her new lawyer clothes, with her round faced baby and smiling husband. Everything in the old place was grey – washed out and used up. She once bought her father some red coffee cups. They strutted like roosters across his counter until they eventually faded from view. 'Drea thought they'd gradually just broken, as crockery would, but last winter she'd found three of them buried in the back of a cupboard. She never had asked Pop why.

'Drea came back to the present with a start. She had managed to get Keisha safely bathed and into her PJs and they were sitting together on the play mat in Keisha's room with a set of toy blocks. The smell of grilled chicken wafted up the stairs, and she heard the screen door and the clatter of dog toes.

"Dinner's up, Dray!" Michael called up the stairs.

"Thanks," she called back. "Be down in a minute." She got Keisha to help her put the blocks in a little bucket and then scooped her up. "Ready to eat, Miss Princess?"

"Ah-HUNH!" Keisha was definitely ready. 'Drea carried her back down the stairs and found Michael had set the table in the dining room. He moved Keisha's high chair over and had even found some cloth napkins. And a silly green candle. It went with nothing else on the table, but it glowed like his heart. He had such a big heart. 'Drea felt some of the ice she'd been harboring shift. In truth she didn't really know why it was there – it just was. But now it was leaving.

He handed her a plate heaped with corn and chicken, then cut up and blew on some chicken for Keisha. When everyone had been served, he poured two plastic tumblers of lemonade – she had forgotten to run the dishwasher, so they were the only clean glasses they had. Michael couldn't have cared less. He gave her a big open smile.

"Cheers, 'Dray – happy fourth anniversary. I think it's the canine anniversary because the universe got us a dog." And then she was laughing and crying at the same time and when he came to her, she hung on like a woman drowning. He just held her and said what he always did, "No worries, lovely. No worries."

When she finally stopped crying, he gave her just one gentle kiss. She smiled at him and wiped her eyes and made a funny face.

"Wait a minute – what fourth anniversary is this?" It wasn't their wedding anniversary, and it wasn't when they met at that baseball game. It wasn't even the anniversary of their first date. Michael grinned at her, a blush coppering his cheeks.

"It's the anniversary of the day Bullet decided we were going to be a family." She put a hand to her mouth and fresh tears welled.

"So now I guess he's telling us our family is growing again…" 'Drea pointed to the two dogs, sitting happily side by side outside the pet gate. Bullet was nuzzling Pirate behind one ear.

71

"One more Manfield joining the team!" Michael laughed and pumped his fist.

She took his hand and smiled and said, "Or two."

11. Find

To the left there were four houses, to the right three more. He looked back and forth several times and still had no idea which one he was supposed to go to. It was one of those developments with a Plan A and a Plan B. Apparently the homeowners here were all A-types. There was almost nothing to distinguish these homes – all had pearl grey siding and darker shutters. They each had a row of shrubs under a large front window. Each had a two-car garage on the left and a postage stamp square of cement as a front stoop. No cars were left out – couldn't tell them apart that way. Each had a cement driveway with a few scraggly weeds poking up through the cracks. The weeds in the fourth one were brown, so Reg figured they'd sprayed with something. He almost celebrated – it was the first difference he'd seen. He was suddenly reminded of those puzzles from childhood, "Spot five differences between these two pictures!" He rubbed his face and smiled under his hand. But he noted it on a scratch pad.

He sat slouched in a blue sedan parked just back from the intersection of Post and Poppy. The area had been hit by violent storms a few weeks back, so the homes he could see across the street were the only occupied ones. Those on the near side of the street had been badly battered by the tornado, several had roofs caved in and they were being torn down. He was supposed to deliver papers to a home on Poppy Lane, but it was a rush job and when he got there he realized he hadn't been given a correct address – all of these houses had two digit numbers, the address he was given had four. And there was no phone number. The name he had didn't match those on any of the mailboxes, either. At least the mailboxes were standing. The last house had no mailbox. Reg put that on his scratch pad, too.

He looked at the papers he was supposed to deliver. Something about a vicious dog. He shrugged. He didn't see any dogs. Five of the homes had fenced yards, chain link, with gates on the side next to the garage. He couldn't see much of the back yards, but didn't see any chewed up toys that might indicate a dog had been in any of them. He could just see a swing set behind the fourth house. He made another note. He scanned the homes again. Then swung his eyes back to number two, caught by a speck of color. Aha! There was a green shrub missing in front of the house. In its place they had planted a rose bush. It had a few pink and white blooms nodding in a light breeze. Another note.

Reg looked down at his list. Mailboxes, roses, and swing sets were not going to get this job done. He sighed. He figured he was going to have to walk around. He didn't like walking around in neighborhoods where he had to serve. It made people nervous. Nervous people were difficult when you were handing them news they didn't want and didn't like. Nervous people sometimes did stupid things. Especially nervous people with supposedly vicious dogs. He shook his head, but he decided to get out of the car anyway.

In Reg's experience, "vicious" dogs seldom were. If something actually happened it would turn out they were provoked, or they were allowed to get into some situation they shouldn't have been in and couldn't get out of, or they were just being dogs. And a lot of the time, all that had happened was a lot of noise. He remembered one guy who got served because his toy poodle always sat in the front window and barked at kids walking home from the school bus. One girl was terrified that the dog monster was going to come get her. Instead of helping the kid figure out how to be OK, the parents decided to blame the dog and sue. The owner didn't even know the dog was doing this – he was always at work and they'd never bothered to contact him. So the first he heard of it was a civil suit. Reg remembered the look on the guy's face. And the poodle that sat calmly in the front hall while Reg delivered the news. Reg vaguely remembered that the case had been thrown out. That judge didn't have any patience for whining.

Reg opened the door and slung his legs out. He eased into a standing position and stretched. The whole place was eerily quiet. A few sparrows chirped from a vacant lot where a battered house had already been torn down. Nothing else moved. He headed left, intending to walk the row of houses from one end to the other. He was halfway across the front of the second vacant lot when he heard a "whoosh!" of heavy breath and he was suddenly on the ground, without a sound, the breath knock out of him. He blinked in surprise and something wet touched his face. He twisted around and looked straight into the face of a St. Bernard.

"Well, hello," Reg spoke softly. The dog was standing over him, with a massive paw on either side of Reg's chest. It was nuzzling the jacket pocket where he'd stashed a candy bar.

"Are you hungry, puppy?" Reg moved his left hand slowly and held it up for the dog to sniff. The dog gave half a sniff to the hand and then returned attention to Reg's pocket. Reg sat up very slowly, scooting himself to give the dog some space.

"I think I can help you with that," Reg kept talking in a low easy voice and stood up slowly. He kept one eye on the dog, and eased his way back to the car with the dog keeping pace, still snuffling at his pocket. Reg put a hand on the trunk and popped the catch. He opened it gradually and reached in for the box of biscuits he always had. He never knew when they might be handy. Like now. In fact, it was pretty dumb that he hadn't gotten a few out before, given what he was here for.

He shook a few biscuits out on the ground and the dog inhaled them in seconds. Reg shook out a few more and watched the repeat. He wondered if this was the "vicious dog". The dog didn't seem dangerous – just hungry. Its coat was spotted with dried mud and some shards of dry grass. He wondered if it had gotten lost in the storms or if someone decided they didn't want to feed it.

"You wanna wait for me here?" He held a hand out to the dog, who sniffed at it, then stretched its head toward the biscuit box. Reg shook out a few more and waited for it to eat. Then he put a biscuit in his flat palm and held it out toward the big muzzle. The biscuit was gently inhaled and a swipe of wet dog tongue left in its place. Reg chuckled to himself. He handed it another biscuit and ventured a very light touch with his other hand. No reaction. So he stroked it gently across the head and it leaned into him. Certainly didn't seem to be the kind of hyper-reactive dog that usually got labeled as vicious. He felt for a collar and found none.

Reg shook his head and unlocked the car. He opened the back door and the dog jumped in even before Reg put a couple more biscuits on the seat. He closed the door, got in the front and turned the key to get power to the windows. He rolled them all down about six inches and got back out.

"I'll be back in a few minutes. Please don't eat my car." The dog cocked its head at him, then went back to sniffing at the seat for biscuit crumbs.

Reg trotted off to make a quick round of the block. He hoped the dog was as mild mannered as it seemed. Now that it was penned in the back of his car. Reg got back to business. At the first two houses there was no one home and there was no sign of a dog's presence in either yard. At the third, an elderly woman answered his knock and stared at him as he asked if she was Mrs. Halliwell. She kept staring, then looked him up and down, muttered, "Too skinny" and simply walked away from the door. Reg stood there for a moment, wondering whether he should try the question again. Then he heard tennis shoes running toward him. A harried young woman in blue scrubs and a white sweater hustled to the door. She looked like she was ready to slam it in his face.

"Hello, miss. Is this the Halliwell residence?" He kept his tone very calm and respectful.

She pushed at one of her sweater sleeves and folded her arms. "No." Hazel eyes were giving him the cold shoulder even as he saw how beautiful they were.

"Could you tell me if there's anyone on the street by that name?"

"Never heard of 'em." She looked back over her shoulder and said, "No, Mom…. Mom, we can't…." as the elderly woman came back carrying a photo.

"You find things, young man?" She looked directly at Reg and spoke in a teacher's voice that brooked no funny business.

"Yes, ma'am. Sometimes," he answered, true enough.

"This is my Howard. He's missing. Find him." She shoved the picture at Reg and walked off again.

Reg looked at the faded Polaroid, at the image of a young man in uniform, next to a young woman and a little girl.

"Your father?" he asked the young woman. She nodded, then reached for the photo. "Not that it's any of your business."

"I'm sorry," he dipped his head, then turned. "I … uh…" It finally occurred to him to ask about the dog. He looked back at her, "Do you know if someone around here has a St. Bernard?"

He fully expected her to say no and close the door. Instead she burst into tears. "I used to. I think she was stolen – she went missing after I broke up with my ex-boyfriend and I spent months looking for her. He wouldn't return my calls or messages. His sister just kept hanging up on me."

"Were you living here when she went missing?"

She nodded. "Wait right here," he said it, hoping that she would.

He turned and jogged down the block back to the car. He got in and slowly pulled it around to the front of the house where she still stood in the door, now with her hand over her mouth as she saw the dog in the back seat. The dog started barking. Reg got out and opened the back door and the dog was out and halfway to the house in a bound.

"Lacey! Lacey!" The young woman was on her knees in the yard, weeping, and hugging the dog who was bouncing and trying to cover her in sloppy kisses. Reg got the box of biscuits out of the car, now slightly chewed, and set it on the porch for her.

"I'm glad you found your dog, miss." He turned to go.

"Wait," she was smiling now, through tears and a generous smudging of St. Bernard hair. "I think Halliwell was the name on one of the houses that had to be torn down. It was Hall-something. They're probably gone."

"Thanks, I'll check that out."

"Where did you find her?"

He pointed back toward the vacant lots, "Just right over there. She toppled me to sniff at a candy bar in my pocket. Didn't have a collar, so I didn't know she was almost home."

She shook her head. "All those months. Oh my God, Lacey!" She held onto the dog as if she would drown in a second without her. A movement caught Reg's eye and he looked up to see the older woman standing on the porch, excited, but hesitating at the steps. He quickly went over and gave her hand to hang on to, then supported her tiny bird elbow as she tottered down the two steps to join her daughter.

"It's the big dog!" she said. "Look at that!" Lacey left off smothering her mistress to gently nuzzle one shaky hand. "Nice dog."

"Yes, she is, Mama. She's the best dog." The younger woman looked up at Reg over the dog's back. "I can't thank you enough. Having her back is such a burden off me. I was so afraid she'd been harmed." New tears flowed down her face.

"I'm glad she's home and happy," Reg didn't know what else to say. He felt like he was intruding on this family and their reunion, so he started to turn back to the car.

"Wait," she said again, struggling to her feet. "I posted a reward for finding her. I owe you that, at least."

"Miss, I couldn't – really. She was less than two blocks away when I found her. She'd have been on your doorstep in minutes if I hadn't put her in the car." The whole thing suddenly struck him as funny. He chuckled.

"What?" She looked confused.

Reg pointed at the dog, "The only thing I've managed to find today is a dog who wasn't lost."

The hazel-eyed woman in the blue scrubs smiled at him and said, "And us." She extended a hand. "I'm Philippa Johnson, and this is my mother, Rose."

"Pleasure, Miss Johnson, ma'am" he shook her hand and smiled at both of them. "Reginald Waithes; just Reg usually."

"Reg, could we offer you a cup of coffee?" He hesitated a moment, but then Rose smiled at him and took his hand and Lacey circled behind him and nudged him with her big head. Reg nodded and was escorted by three lovely ladies into a small house suddenly like no other.

⊱⊰ ⊱⊰ ⊱⊰ ⊱⊰ ⊱⊰

12. Beginning

"This isn't hard," Kiko thought. "It is very strange, but it isn't hard." It was odd to have an almost-hurt in places that didn't usually hurt. But that seemed far away because of what came with the almost-hurt. There was the hurt and then there was a tiny warm creature, born of her body, needing to nuzzle, and she nuzzled. Kiko licked and nuzzled the first tiny bundle, then a second, and a third. They inched forward and found her belly and latched on. She grew warm and content and her babies grew round. This was meant to be so.

Kiko slept, waking once to issue a stern warning to Laser, who came sniffing around with that "what's this?" look on his feline face. For once he backed off and she went back to sleep. The humans came and went, the smaller ones squealing softly and the big ones reaching in to touch her. She lifted her head and one corner of her lip. She was not ready for hands. She accepted a small plate of food and a little water. She tended the brood. Finally, when she could no longer put it off, she gently untangled her legs from the sleeping whelps and tucked the soft blanket around them, issued a stern warning to Laser, and got her favorite human to let her into the yard. Kiko rushed to the proper spot, went quickly and ran back to the door.

She had to scratch for a minute to be let back in, panic rising in her chest. The other tall human finally opened the door and she ran to her babies. Muzzle - one, belly - two, little tail – three. All safe. Kiko curled around them, shivering slightly. When a smaller human came up, she turned her head and issued a warning. A bigger small one took that one away and she relaxed. One half-awake pup began rooting against her belly, she nudged it with her muzzle to the right place and he took hold. Soon they were all nursing and she floated in a strange and lovely place between sleeping and waking, being safe and being alert, being a One and being a part of Many. She felt unafraid, yet alert to danger. It was in her bones to protect these tiny sucklings from any possible harm. Even the humans she knew and loved. These babies had no questions yet, so neither did Kiko. Things were as they were.

She vaguely remembered the dog who fathered them. She had been in season and he had sensed and come courting. She saw him twice for the wandering season and then not again for a time. When he came next he was changed and there would be no other pups with one blue eye and a curly tail. Two of her litter would have their sire's wild blue eye. The humans didn't know this yet. It would be some days before the pups would be ready to see the world. Kiko did not mark the time – she just knew that there was a season and it would come. Her only job now was to suckle and protect. So she did.

Time had a pulse but little presence in the nursery. Kiko slept alongside her young, and nuzzled and groomed them. She nudged them to her belly to nurse and made sure each fed well. She ate and drank from the bowls the humans brought to her. She slept in the sun, and left the puppies only to make her toilet outside. She would come straight back and nuzzle each little creeping body. Slowly, the pups began to gain size and strength. They squealed more loudly at each other and at her. They suckled of her and grew their bodies, snouts and paws and legs and tails. First one little male, then the other opened his eyes and greeted their dam. The little girl was last, savoring her waited-for being. Like one of her brothers, she had a mischievous blue-black stare, one light side, one dark side. Their dark-eyed brother favored Kiko, except for the extravagant curl of his tail. All of the whelps had their father's bandit face and Kiko's long legs.

The smaller humans came to stare for hours on end. Gradually, as the pups grew stronger and began to walk, Kiko let the humans touch. It seemed the natural order to allow these hands more latitude as her little ones became more adventurous. They would live with ones like these. Maybe these even. Kiko did not know. She cared – but there was no way for her to know where her babies would be in the time when they were babies no more. It was her job to grow them until they were able to eat well without her. She gave herself to that. The time after was not now.

The sun rose and fell, the moon grew large and then thinned. The pups grew taller and stronger. They were a unit, twelve legs running, three muzzles busy, three tails happy. They went with Kiko to the yard now, prancing around her and bouncing away to play with one of the humans. They were now old enough to realize there was a world beyond their mother and its mantle was not tied to her shoulders. She watched them with pride, these creatures new of body, who came from her body. She had fulfilled the covenant. There were paws to strike the earth and noses to take the air and voices to fill the sky when her risings and settings were done. Kiko watched her puppies play and stood tall.

13. Pack

"Four days," she muttered. "That's all I gotta get through. Four days." Sheila threw another cotton top into the suitcase lying open on her bed, followed by a pair of khaki pants. She rummaged in the bottom of the closet and found a pair of sandals, which she tossed toward the open suitcase. One landed in it. The other skidded over a corner and she heard it hit the floor.

"awENH!"

Or maybe not the floor. "Sorry, BooBoo! Didn't mean to hit you." She walked around the bed to the old basset hound looking up at her with a long face. Of course, bassets always had a long face – but age made Bongo's even longer. His long muzzle was grey and white hair flecked the ears that had been all brown. They still swept the floor. And he still sounded like a foghorn when he bayed. He just did it less frequently. Everything was less frequent now. Sheila leaned forward to stroke his head.

"You're a good boy, Bongo-boo."

She usually didn't mind travel but she hated having to go away, hated to leave him behind, especially now that he was getting crotchety. The to-do list for the pet sitter got longer and longer every time she had to go somewhere. He had a pill for his arthritis. His food was for senior dogs. He needed to be let out more often because it was hard for him to wait for over six hours. There was one spot on his back where he didn't like to be touched. He needed help getting his considerable bulk up onto the couch next to her. He was so long a stepstool didn't help, he couldn't get his front feet and his back feet on it at the same time. And at 65 pounds, he was not the lightest dog to lift. She had to do half of him at a time, which he allowed, but she could tell it annoyed him.

He was fairly tolerant of Priscilla, who was six months old and mischievous; he would let her play with his tail and even smack at his ears. Sheila could tell he knew this creature wasn't Regan, her sweet old torti who used to curl up with him, but it was somehow related. Regan had died peacefully in her sleep last year. Sheila had adopted Priscilla a few months ago, wanting a cat, and unable to resist her orneriness. Pris was now bigger than Regan and more active and she didn't recognize "no" as an answer to anything. Sheila kept meaning to have a conversation with her about that. Really. Sometimes "no" actually was the answer. Especially when it came to Sheila's shoes. Sheila had to explain to people that, no, the dog hadn't chewed her shoes, the cat had played with them.

Sheila looked down at Bongo; he was half-sitting up, ears just barely off the floor. He was giving her that special basset look: nose down, eyes up, lower lids drooping. The Eeyore look. *Aw, you noticed me. By waking me up. Now I have to go pee, and that means I have to stand up. And walk all the way down the hall, and then out the door. Oh, you patted my head. Thanks. That's nice. I still have to get up and walk.*

She watched with a small smile as he heaved himself to his feet and began the long trek down the hall. She followed and opened the sliding door for him. He lumbered onto the deck, then down the two steps to the yard. She'd had them lengthened and widened for him some years ago, so he had room for his big paws and long body. He still went down them fairly well. Up anything was becoming hard for him. Heave, lumber, heave, sigh. He was back at her feet, looking at her with blame in his face, having briefly forayed into the yard to pee. She realized the grass was getting a bit high and this was his complaint. As if to underscore that, he slowly shook his big head, trying to dry the tips of his ears, wet with dew. She would have to call the Mary Rogers and see if Seth would come over to mow. One more thing to do before she left.

Shelia smiled and knelt to pet him. "Aw, sorry, big guy. Did those ears get wet? Aw!" She watched him partly forgive her. "OK, bud. Let's get your breakfast." He followed her back into the house, pausing briefly to sniff at Priscilla, who was lounging in her basket by the big sliding door, washing her face. Pris liked a view of all proceedings. And she liked Bongo. Sheila watched as the cat rubbed her head on Bongo's nose and the sweetness of a happy fur family welled in her chest. There was a little spark of sadness there. Bongo was nearing his tenth birthday. She reached down to pet both of them.

They were so precious to her. She didn't have kids, didn't know what that was like, but she would fight long, mean, and dirty for her pets. They were her family. Woe betide the idiot who thought they were "just animals". She was legendary in her old job at the library for absolutely destroying the guy who kicked a stray dog on the sidewalk out front. She had been out the door and down the steps so fast she seemed to just appear, eyes flaming, almost spitting fury. He backed up so fast he fell over the curb then scrambled to his feet and ran off. She'd never said a word. The dog slunk over to her ankles and she gently felt along its skinny back and piano key ribs. She had taken it to her own vet and one of the techs adopted it. Today he was a sleek, happy family dog.

So Pris and Bongo really were her family. There were days she wanted to do nothing more than just sit with them, nap with the dog, play with the cat; eat sleep play dream.

"Yeah," she said aloud. She had no idea how to make that happen. But she could make breakfast happen. "That'll do for now."

Bongo was sitting with his head hanging over his food dish. He swung his head slowly, eyes following her as she scooped his kibble from the bin and filled the bowl for him. She tossed in a couple soft treats and he seemed to nod at her before tucking into it. She topped up Pris's bowl with a little extra cat food and then hit the button on the coffee pot. She'd set that up the night before and just hadn't started it yet.

She poured some cereal into a bowl and sniffed at a carton of milk. She made a face and poured it out in the sink. "Eesh! Tha's nasty." She was muttering to herself again, not really even loud enough that she could say she was talking to the animals, who weren't listening, anyway.

Going back to the fridge, Sheila found little cup of plain yogurt that was still good and dumped that into her cereal. Not exactly what she'd been going for, but not bad. A beep from the coffee pot alerted her to the proximity of caffeine; she poured a large mug, took a big swig, and almost moaned in relief. She sat at the counter to eat and for a few minutes they all munched in companionable silence. Pris just nibbled a little for quality assurance and then wandered back to her spot in the sun to continue her morning wash up. Bongo slowly and carefully chased each bit of kibble around his bowl until he had captured them all. Then he got a big sloppy drink, dousing his ears again. He shook them off, spraying Sheila's legs, and went to snore contentedly on his big bed in the den.

Sheila dabbed at her wet ankles with a kitchen towel, then got another cup of coffee and took it back to the bedroom to continue packing. She caught a glimpse of herself in the full-length mirror. "Good lord." She was muttering again. She looked like a puppet in a Tim Burton movie. Her streaky blond hair was doubled into a ponytail and then piled on her head, with ends flying everywhere. Her round glasses made her look child-like, an effect emphasized by the thinness of her wrists and ankles, sticking out of her pajamas. She had always been this way. Her high school nickname was "Stork", even though she wasn't particularly tall, she was just thinner than most people her height. One too-clever boy even called her Ichabod Jane. That one stuck for a while, until they moved on to something else in English class.

She rolled her eyes and shook her head, shaking off that little trip down memory lane. She was about to go on a four-day trip; she needed to figure out what to pack besides one pair of khakis and a shirt. She fell back on the obvious – one pair of navy pants, a little dressed down, and one pair of black trousers, a little dressed up. She put in a few tops that could go with either pair, and a black and white houndstooth blazer. Navy skirt. One pair of flats she could walk in, one pair of heels, in case things got too fancy. Done!

She was about to close the suitcase when Priscilla hopped into it and started circling to find to softest spot. Sheila bit back a sharp comment as she realized that Pris was saving her ass – maybe literally. She'd been so focused on the other stuff she'd forgotten underwear and pajamas.

"Gawd!" she scolded herself instead. She got out the usual "plus one" day's worth of underwear and a pair of soft PJs – oh! – and some socks! – and then put her little toiletry kit on the pile.

She looked at it all. And at Pris now sound asleep in her luggage, curled into a contented C, with her legs stretched and a self satisfied little feline smile. "Too precious," Sheila muttered. She sat down on the bed, in part intending to scoop the cat into her arms. But she didn't. She reached over and caressed the cat. Then she stood up and trotted into the other room to check on Bongo.

He was sound asleep, perfectly happy. Sheila realized how suddenly scared she'd felt when it went away. And she thought, *I don't want this. I don't want to leave him. I don't want him to be alone with a stranger coming in and out, while I get on and off planes and in and out of meetings in an effort to impress people I will never meet again over something I couldn't care less about. Right here, right now – he's what I care about and I don't want to leave him.*

"So why am I?"

"What the…?" Sheila sat down on the couch with a thump. Most of the time she didn't think about what she did for work – she just did it.

"And maybe that's the problem." She rolled her eyes and waved both hands. "And isn't this just the time to be realizing it."

She was supposed to be on a plane in three hours. She thought for a moment about not going and not saying anything. And then realized that was dumb. This trip was supposed to be a perk and there were two other people from work going. They would certainly notice she wasn't there. She could just say she was ill – though that wasn't true and she had no stomach for lying. Though it would not be wrong to say she was indisposed. She was. She was entirely indisposed. It would not be her fault if they assumed one meaning while she most certainly meant another.

"Oh, Sheila, you are evil," she told herself. But she felt lighter than she had all day. She practically twirled back to the bedroom chanting, "Indisposed! Indisposed!" She was grinning madly.

"Guess what, Pris?" she asked the cat who had woken up and was yawning at her. "You're off the hook – you can sleep in there all day if you want." Eat sleep play dream.

Sheila was going to try that herself. She almost skipped to the phone.

🐈🐈🐈🐈🐈

14. If

"If you were a dog, what kind would you be?"

Marina looked at him. Had this cracker lost his mind? Aloud she said, "What?!" implying the other two words with her tone and the look on her face.

James just smiled and repeated himself. Carefully. Knowing this would push every button he'd missed the first time.

"If. You. Were. A. Dog. What kind. Would you. Be?"

She rolled her eyes. But the rule was, she had to play along. So she made a face and said the first thing that came to mind. "Something big enough to be scary, but cute enough to be lovable."

"What kind would that be?""

"Whatever kind. You know – about so high," she laid a hand flat in the air just above her knee. "And so long," she held her hands out, a little wider than her shoulders. "And I like the ones with pointy ears. They just look smarter."

"Do you want to BE smarter? Or just look it?"

She gave him a look that said he was close to the danger zone. "OK, we'll grant that you'd be a smart dog."

She just pressed her lips together and didn't reply.

"What color would you be as a dog?"

"Dogs don't get to choose their color – they just are. Brownish, blackish, a little white. But if I did get to choose, I'd want those little spots over each eye."

"And you'd have dark eyes?"

"No, blue eyes. Like those wicked smart cattle dogs. Or huskies." For a moment she was almost hooked on the game. And then she sat back and studied her nails.

"Would you have short or long hair?"

"Medium long... ish." She was being deliberately vague. "Not like those mop dogs, but not like a Weimaraner, either." She shrugged. "Long enough and thick enough to like winter."

"Where would you want to live as a dog?"

"Some place I could have plenty of room to run and play." In her mind, she saw a mountain retreat, meadows and woods and freedom.

"But not with people?"

"With the right people. People who would be kind and loving. Who would feed me good food and have a safe place for me to sleep at night. And maybe they'd have other dogs, too. So we could all run and play."

"You'd have a pack?"

"Kind of. But the people would be in the pack, too."

"So you would protect them, too?"

"If they were good to me and I loved them."

"And if they weren't good to you?"

"That would be sad. Dogs deserve better."

"And you, too?"

She looked at him, blank-faced. This idea hit her squarely between the eyes, burrowed in and lodged in her brain. Holy. Crap.

"I... oh my God..." her voice trailed off. She saw, now, where he'd been headed. Now that she was sitting, trussed, on the doorstep.

"Shit, James. That was dirty pool."

He gave her the same mild smile he always had. "Not at all. Just following the metaphor." He paused to let her take it in.

"So, are we in agreement that Marina-the-dog and Marina-the-person BOTH deserve to be treated well, simply because they are living beings and living beings should be treated well?"

She shrugged and nodded at the same time.

"That was equivocal," he observed.

She wanted to smack the self-satisfied little smile off his face. But she knew it would solve nothing. She pulled from an inner well of strength. And protective sarcasm.

"Yes, living beings deserve to be treated well. Even the annoying ones." She stuck her tongue out at him.

His face didn't change and he made a notation on the legal pad he was holding on his crossed knee. It took all she had to stay in her chair.

He waited for a long half minute, then said, "Well done."

She gave him a look that was the equivalent of showing him one finger.

"But you're still here. You're not in tears, in my face, or out the door. This is progress."

She gave him a hard stare, but eventually nodded. She wasn't going to give him the satisfaction of a verbal agreement.

He nodded and looked down at the pad. "Continuing," his glasses were down on his nose as he flipped back one page in his notes. "If you were this dog, where would your safe, happy, free home be?"

"With my pack, people ones and dog ones."

"And what sort of place would it be in?" He gestured, indicating the world.

"Hunh?" She knew what he meant; she was just stalling. Revealing that she immediately thought of a mountain cabin on a lake seemed too much.

His eyes drilled into her. "You know." He waited her out. She stared at her fingernails with veiled eyes and considered how much to disclose and how. Then she looked out the window at the distance.

"Away, you know. Not in a city. No place where the ground is only cement and tiny little holes for little bitty trees. Some place with air to breath and space to run. Some place wide and big-hearted."

She stopped, surprised at what had come out of her mouth.

He was sitting very still, almost holding his breath. Finally he spoke, more quietly than before, "What does a big-hearted place look like?"

"Wide open – you can see a long ways and what you see is beautiful. It is calm and peaceful and green in the summer and white in the winter. Plenty of sun. Enough water."

"And what does it feel like?"

"Open and free. You can breathe. As if mistakes don't matter. Nothing matters but being with your pack and having a full belly and room to roam and a place of your own to sleep."

He looked her full in the face and leaned forward again. "What mistakes don't matter?"

"Any of them," her breath came out ragged. "It just doesn't matter. Dogs don't hang on to grudges, or something you did two years, or two decades, ago. They barely hang on to something from an hour ago. It goes away. Everyone gets a do-over." Tears slid down her cheeks, though she didn't seem to notice.

"Marina," his voice was so soft she had to lean forward to hear him. "If you were a person would you want to live in that same place?"

She gave him the look again. "I am a person!"

"Yes," he nodded. "And would you want to live in that place?"

Even knowing the question was coming, she was still nonplussed. Of course, she wanted to live there, who didn't?

"Well, yes. It'd be dumb not to." She was impatient again.

"Is this that place?"

She shook her head, "No way."

"What would make a place 'that' place?"

She stared at a middle distance. She had no idea if the place she described was open to her.

"It's… It would have to… I don't know how to get there…" She looked at him, without pretense, without defense. "I don't know."

"You do," he said it gently. "You just told me."

"That's a 'place'," she made quotes with her fingers. "You're talking about making it appear and I don't know how to do that."

He was quiet a moment. Then spoke slowly.

"What would you feel like in that place?"

"At home." The tears came again. "Welcomed. My best self. Unafraid. Un… unen…cumbered." She stumbled a little on the word.

"What else?"

She grabbed at a tissue and wiped her eyes, started to say "I don't know" and stopped, knowing that wouldn't work.

"I could be happy there, maybe not all the time – but it could happen."

"How will you recognize that place when you find it?"

"When?" she smirked at him. "You're an optimist."

He gestured to her, "Humor me."

She made a face, but went on, "It will feel like home. My feet will know when they touch it. I felt that once – years ago. Not here. Before, y'know?"

He nodded.

She was gesturing now, pulling her closed hands to her chest, then opening them, palm up in front of her. "I'd feel like I could live in my skin and not worry about being judged for it. I'd be able to make a life and a living. It would matter to me." She looked down, then up again. "I would matter."

"To you?"

"To me," she said softly. "To somebody."

"Who, Marina?"

"To Tay."

"You miss Tay." It wasn't a question.

She nodded, tears flowing again. "I know that's dumb, after all that happened. I'm an idiot for thinking it would even be reasonable for me to go back. But it's the only relationship I've ever had where someone thought I was worth something."

"What did he think you were worth, Marina?" They had been over this ground before.

"About a hundred-fifty an hour. Sometimes more if the guy wanted to get rough." She was deliberately blunt, smacking herself in the face with it more than him.

"And what did you get out of that?"

"A place to sleep. Decent food. Sometimes. Some cocaine now and then. Clothes and make-up to keep the clients happy. And when he was nice to me, it was really nice."

"And when things weren't so good, what about then?"

"I got used. Smacked around. A lot of bruises in bad places. Couldn't go anywhere without his say-so. No warm clothes. Too little money of my own to buy more than a pack of cigarettes."

"What got you out?" He knew. But he knew she had to say it.

"Got beat up for not letting a guy hurt me. He wouldn't pay and Tay was pissed. Pushed me so hard I tripped over a coffee table, fell. It knocked me out and my head was bleeding. Scared Kiki to death, so she took me to the ER. It was the nurse who figured out what was what. Called the cops. Chewed the guy out when he tried to arrest me for prostitution. Said, 'this girl ain't the criminal, you asshole! Go get the guy who beat her!' Wouldn't let them near me after that."

"Why'd she do that?"

"She ... she said, 'Honey, you're too young to pour your life down that drain. You're worth more than what some jerk is paying some other jerk to use you.' She meant it." She was staring at nothing, seeing and hearing it again. She touched the thin scar at her hairline.

"What else did she do?"

"Found my parents. Called to tell them I was all right. My father told her they'd thrown me out and why would they care about their ungrateful spawn who wouldn't marry the fine man he'd chosen for me. She hung up on him. Came back and told me I needed a clean break in life."

"So she thought you were worth something."

"Yes." The answer was soft, but clear.

"Was she right?"

"Yes."

"So what are you going to do about that?"

She shook her head, "Find somewhere wide and big-hearted? I don't know. I don't know where that is and I don't know how to get there." She was worn out and just wanted to curl up somewhere safe for a while.

He saw her eyes move back and forth, he waited.

"I want to stay someplace safe for a while. Just ...be, y'know?"

"How long has it been since you stayed someplace safe, Marina?"

She shook her head again. "Wow – I don't even know. I was probably six or seven. At my grandma's house. She was real small and real sweet and she used to call me Little Bird." She paused, remembering.

"I haven't thought of that in years. She died not long after that and there weren't any more visits. That's when Mom got sad and Dad got mean." She paused a moment, her eyes went dark and hard. "I was only sixteen when they

97

tried to marry me off to some nasty asshole in his forties. Some guy my father knew, maybe Dad owed him money, I don't know. I hated the son-of-a-bitch. Hated being near him, hated the way he looked at me, hated it when he would rub my face, like he was polishing some shiny toy. He was disgusting."

She stopped and stared at the floor, face contorted as if the taste of the words in her mouth poisoned her. "He was the first guy who hit me. Dad sent us out on a 'date' and he tried to kiss me and I ducked. He punched me and I ran. Got home by walking several miles, then thumbing a ride. When I got home, Dad was waiting up for me, yelling about how I was screwing up and this was a fine, well-off, upstanding businessman. Then he tried to grab my hair and I just ran into my room and locked the door. My mother sat on the couch crying, through the whole thing; never said a word. I threw a few things into my backpack and got out the window just as he kicked the door in. Haven't seen them since."

She looked at her hands and took a breath. "I worry about my mother some. I think it's pretty bad for her; she always backed him up, but she'd try to soften it, make things a little easier. Not always better. She hides the gin bottles."

He nodded.

"What's going to get your feet under you?"

She shrugged, "Finding a way to make a living while upright?"

"Are you asking?"

"No," she sighed. "Just wondering." She lifted one hand, then let it drop, "I don't even know what I'm qualified for. I never even finished high school." Her voice dropped so he barely heard the last part. Though he knew.

"Are there things you thought you would do?"

She nodded, eyes far away. "I actually wanted to be a farm veterinarian. Work with dogs and cows and horses. That visit with Granny – her neighbor was a farmer. I loved

98

all the animals. We never had pets. Dad never wanted anything 'dirty' in the house."

She looked down at her hands and then up at him. "Actually, I think he just didn't want any competition for attention. He's a selfish bastard."

Then she flung up her hands in frustration, "Oh, who am I kidding?! How the hell would I get to be a veterinarian? Just wave my magic wand?"

"Why wouldn't it be possible?"

She named them on her fingers, voice dripping with sarcasm. "Well, James, I don't have a high school diploma. So I can't get into college. Can't pay for college anyway. No college degree – can't go to vet school. Screwed before I start."

"Marina, you don't have to swallow the elephant whole."

She gave him the "what the…?" look again.

"Nobody does all of that at once. What comes first?"

"Finding a way to finish high school, I guess. Though I don't think they let 21-year-old ex-prossies in there."

"You can take a high school equivalency exam."

"Doesn't that look bad?"

"No – it's as valid as a four-year diploma. And you might not have to. Some universities will accept students without it."

She snorted at him, "Right – we'll just put my work experience on the application. Is that considered phys ed or sex ed? Maybe performance art?"

He laughed in spite of himself. "I think you could probably just choose "other" and leave it at that."

"Ya think?" Her eyes brightened and she almost smiled, leavening the air for just a moment. He could sense her mood deflating again.

"It isn't impossible, Marina."

"Isn't exactly easy."

"No, it's not that either. It's just a choice. One you could make, or you could make another. The point is – you get to pick."

She looked at him a little sideways. He didn't usually get preachy.

"Don't go all Disney on me, James. You'll ruin your reputation."

He laughed. "I'm not going to tell you *what* to pick. You're still gonna have to suck it up."

"Well," she smirked again, "and hasn't that been the problem all along."

He had been taking a sip of water and nearly sprayed it across the room.

She laughed out loud. And then they both sat, startled.

"Wow," she spoke so quietly he barely heard her.

"How long has it been since you laughed? Really laughed."

She was shaking her head, "I don't even know." She looked around. "I feel weird, like I might be sore tomorrow because some muscles got a workout that I haven't used in a while."

He was nodding and shaking his head at the same time.

"That's crazy, hunh?" For once she was speaking without prompting.

"But – it felt nice. Like something came loose and a big chunk of rust on the axle came off and now I can roll."

"So where do you want to roll to?"

"The pound," she jumped a little as she said it, startled it had come out of her mouth. But it was true. Her eyes shifted back and forth, as if she saw something new and was trying to take it in.

"And…?" He waited to see where she was going with it.

"I'm going to volunteer," she stopped and looked out the window. "And one day the right dog will show up and I'm going to bring it home and we're going to find the place where we both belong."

- - -

He only saw her once after that day, the week she was discharged. He thought about it when he got the envelope eight months later. The postmark said Montana; there was no return address, no note, just a photograph: Marina in shorts and a t-shirt, sitting on log at a rocky overlook with forested slopes around her, one arm around a blue-eyed black and white husky with a red bandana collar.

15. Owning Up

Some mornings are a little crazier than you can stand: the older cat wants to sit on your chest and purr while the younger one is hurking up something in the hall; the older dog is whining from the living room and the younger one is racing back and forth, annoying both cats and yipping because she HAS. TO. PEE. NOW. Some might wonder why one person needs four pets, and the question is fair, but the answer is "because they arrived". When the Universe hands you a gift, you don't say, No thanks. You give thanks and get on with it.

So gifts they are. Gifts that leave various gifts of their own on the rug, and shed copiously and require food, toys, treats, and beds. And most of them sleep with you anyway, curling up with a chin on your knee or your side, or both. You wake up in the middle of the night, hot and contorted, and when you tug on the lump poking you in the back, you realize that the dog has brought every toy she cares about into the bed and "buried" it under a fleece throw. You just shove it aside and go back to sleep. There are worse things than having two tennis balls, a few ragged stuffed toys, a bone bigger than your fist, and a squeaky bird in the bed.

Small faces greet you each morning, wriggling closer for the ever important first snuggle of the day. This is usually seconds before the hallway pee dance. God forbid you would ever sleep naked because some mornings you barely have time to shove your feet into slippers before you clip the little stinker onto a leash and get her out the door. This one has earned the name "Pogo Shark" for her habit of leaping up and nipping at whatever body part she reaches when she's in a hurry to get out. She is impossible – impossibly cute and seriously opinionated. She does not hesitant to share said opinions, either. She's a pistol and barely bigger than one.

Her older brother, who outweighs her eight-fold and yet allows her to be a complete pest, is the calm one in the family. He's a lolloping hound; she is a jackshund, a flammable mix of Jack Russell and dachshund, otherwise known as The Terrier-ist. Together they are silly and irresistible. She jumps in his face and he just lifts his head up. Until he's had enough and then he pins her with a paw and starts licking her ears. Well, her whole head. He is as good-natured as she is a firecracker. She sits in his "lap" when they are both tired and it's the cutest thing you've ever seen: A tiny white dog with black and brown spots sitting between the paws of a big black hound, leaning against his chest. He'll eventually put his head on one paw and she'll curl up on the other one and they'll fall asleep. It's so cute you stop everything to stare at them for the entire ten minutes they are actually quiet.

They will both use every trick at their disposal to get treats, walks, and attention. They would happily accept full-time attendance, being pack animals and happiest when the pack is together. The only time the little one will slip away is when she is protecting her favorite toys from her brother. Or when it's raining and she hates to poop in the rain, so she will sneak off and do it somewhere in your house that you eventually find. Often you find it because the cat is trying to cover it up with something equally inappropriate. This is not pleasing. But she already knows this and is hiding by the desk chair where she thinks you can't see her, and you can't do more than speak sternly, anyway. Even if all you say is her name, without inflection, she flops on her back wagging just the tip of her tail and lowers her head and looks up at you. The doggy "oops, I'm sorrrreeeeee" look. And so you pick her up gently and she shakes in your arms as you carry her outside and let her walk around for a few minutes. And you wonder, who had her before you found her and what happened that makes her so scared.

She was doing the same flop and wag when you found her, on a cold December afternoon, on a stretch of road with no houses, she had no collar, no tags. You saw something white bouncing along the side of the road and could not tell what this creature was. So you stopped and looked. And it was a small white dog wriggling in the leaf litter and she came right to you, so you scooped her up and she shook for half an hour. So you hung on. And you still are. No one claimed her, no one looked for her, and your cat adopted her, so she is yours. And you are hers. Within days she is every bit as in possession of you as the two cats and the big dog, who let out a squall when you walked in with her and would not quit until he got to give her a proper hello sniff. She is here because she is meant to be. She even knew her name within two days.

This is a dog so adorable the usual greeting from humans meeting her for the first time is "AAAAWWWWWWWW!" This is now referred to as the Chiquita chorus. She gets cold and tired and falls asleep under a coat on your shoulder at a New Year's Eve party. Awwwwww. She bounds in ridiculous arcs over snow taller than she is chasing clumps of snow thrown by your shovel as you try to clear the drive way. She loves snow more than the big dog. Awwwwww. She prances with her tail at a ridiculous angle, constantly moving as long as she's happy, and it waves like an antenna when she's bowing at the cat. Awwwww. She tucks it and skitters around the house getting the big dog to chase her. Awwww. She looks up at you from a nest in the middle of your bed, blankets pulled and piled around her, bat ears flung wide, paws up, willing you to rub her belly. And you do. Awwwww.

She's just cute. And you can't get around that. You don't really even want to. Even though she exasperates you when accidents happen and makes you late for work when she climbs into your lap with the cat and they both fall asleep. You melt to complete mush. They are both too precious for words, adopting you and each other, creating this warm circle of breath and love. You finally know the meaning of "home". And this is where you – and they – belong.

🐐🐐🐐🐐🐐

16. For Jesse

It was a crisp fall day. She sat in the sun, enjoying the warmth that rose in her body to meet it. The air was easy to breathe. She felt lighter. The other wanted her to go inside, but she refused. This sun needed her now. She laid her head on her paws to let it fall on her neck and sighed one sigh. Sun touched her and she was warm and the air felt like the softest bed. Weariness gave way to a light sleep and she gave herself to the sun.

She felt the touch of the other's hand on her head, but she didn't move. She was content. She felt the other's love and she loved the other. She would carry the lightest parts with her. She was readying for a journey the other could not make. She felt the pull of the sun, warmth and energy giving ease to her body. The spirit within her heard the song of the moon, distant, growing closer, an invitation to join. She had sung those songs here. They became part of her. Now she would become part of them.

The sun gave her warmth and she returned the same. The moon gave her song and she returned the same. The other gave her love and she returned the same. The earth gave her life and she would return the same. She had no fear, only peace. Day swung toward evening and the stars began to lift.

She rose and took a few steps to the place she slept most often and laid there one last time. She felt the body leave her as the other wept. She gave what blessing she could. Freedom beckoned and she answered. And rose to become one with the great song.

Sit.

Stay.

Read.

Good dog.